A Step from Heaven

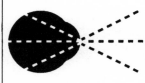

This Large Print Book carries the
Seal of Approval of N.A.V.H.

A Step from Heaven

An Na

Thorndike Press • Waterville, Maine

Published in 2002 by arrangement with Front Street, Inc.

Thorndike Press Large Print Young Adult Series.

The tree indicium is a trademark of Thorndike Press.

The text of this Large Print edition is unabridged.
Other aspects of the book may vary from the original edition.

Set in 16 pt. Plantin by Rick Gundberg.

Printed in the United States on permanent paper.

Library of Congress Cataloging-in-Publication Data

Na, An, 1972–
  A step from heaven / An Na.
    p. cm.
  Summary: A young Korean girl and her family find it
difficult to learn English and adjust to life in America.
    ISBN 0-7862-4126-8 (lg. print : hc : alk. paper)
    1. Korean Americans — Juvenile fiction. 2. Large type
books. [1. Korean Americans — Fiction. 2. Family life —
Fiction. 3. Emigration and immigration — Fiction. 4. Large
type books.] I. Title.
PZ7.N1243 St 2002
  [Fic]—dc21   2002016034

For my mother and father

Acknowledgments

My deepest gratitude to the Mesa Refuge Foundation for the gift of time and space. To Jacqueline Woodson, Norma Fox Mazer, Sharon Darrow, and Brock Cole at the Vermont College MFA in Writing Children's Literature Program, your knowledge and unwavering support brought this book into the light. To Jennifer Brown, James Nagle, Harriet Muir, Deborah Drickersen Cortez, and Ian Haney Lopez, those amazing dinners and fits of laughter were the best endings to my days. And to my editor, Stephen Roxburgh, thank you for rendering the words anew.

Sea Bubble

Just to the edge, Young Ju. Only your feet. Stay there.

Cold. Cold water. Oh. My toes are fish. Come here. Fast. Look.

What is it, Young Ju?

See my toes. See how they are swimming in the sea? Like fish.

Yes, they are little fat piggy fish.

Ahhh! Tickles.

Come on. Up. Keep your legs around me. Are you ready to go swim in the waves?

Hold me. Hold me.

I have you. Look over there, Young Ju. See how the waves dance. See? Hold on tight. We are going over there.

No. Stop. Deep water. Go back.

Shhh, Young Ju. Do not be afraid. You must learn how to be brave. See, I have you.

No. No. Go back.

Young Ju, can you be brave? Look, that is only a small wave. Do not worry. I will hold you tight the whole time. Can you try to be a brave girl for me?

I will try.

Good girl. Ready for the wave? Here it comes. Get ready. Up. And down. There, do you still want to go back?

Again. Do it again. Another one.

That is my courageous girl. Hold on to my neck, Young Ju. Here we go. Up. And down.

I am a sea bubble floating, floating in a dream. Bhop.

All This Weight

Apa is not happy.

Uhmma is not happy.

Halmoni, who is old and has a sleepy blanket face, says that a long time ago Apa was young like me and she could boss him around. But not anymore.

Now, Halmoni can only shake her head when Apa comes home late stinking like the insides of the bottles that get left on the street. Her lips pinch tight, then she hides with Uhmma and me. Because when Apa is too quiet with the squinty eye, it is better to hide until he falls asleep or else there will be breaking everywhere. Halmoni always says, That Apa of yours needs a good spanking. If only your Harabugi had not passed away.

But sometimes when Uhmma is tired of playing sleep, she stops hiding. I pull on her arm. Try to make her get back under the covers. Uhmma shakes away my hand. She slides back the rice paper doors. Her voice deep as night asks, Where were you?

I hide under the covers because the breaking is too loud, too strong. It can come inside my head even though my fingers are in my ears. It sits in my chest, hitting, hitting my heart until my eyes bleed water from the sea. Halmoni rocks me in her lap. Talks to Harabugi's picture. She tells him, Do you see what is happening? How could you leave me with all this weight?

Only God Can

Pray, Halmoni says. Pray to God and everything will be better. Put your hands together tight like a closed book. Good. Then say what I taught you, Young Ju. Remember? Dear Father who art in heaven.

Halmoni, where is heaven?

Heaven is where your Harabugi is. He is with God in a place where there is only goodness and love.

Can I go there?

Someday. If you pray and love God. Do you love God?

Yes, I say, even though at church the picture of his face with the dark round money eyes makes me hide behind the bench. But I want to see heaven and Harabugi, so I try to love him.

Is heaven around here? Can we go there tomorrow? I ask.

No, no. Heaven is in the sky and far away. Now pray while I read the Good Book.

I close my eyes and put my hands together tight. I move my lips the way I see Halmoni do, but without the sounds. God must have very strong ears to hear the words.

Dear Father in heaven.

This is all I remember, so I open my eyes. Halmoni is rocking and reading her Good Book with all the stories about how God came down to be with us. Only when he got here, he said his name was Jesus. I wonder, why did he make up a new name? I wish I could make up a new name, but Halmoni says, Do not be foolish.

I look at Harabugi's picture on the table with the candles all around. He has sleepy eyes like cats in the sun. They are nice eyes. My Harabugi. Apa has the same eyes. Also the same black hair sticking up straight in the front and flat in the back. I close my eyes and put my hands together tight.

Harabugi, I say with my lips moving but without the sound, if you are in heaven with God maybe you can hear me too. Halmoni says Apa needs a good spanking and there is nobody here to give him one. Could you send God down so he can be Jesus again and give Apa his spanking? Then Apa will be nice all the time. Like when he brought home Mi Shi and Uhmma said, We cannot keep that dog. And Apa said, But she is only a baby doggy. Then he made the baby-doggy face. And Uhmma laughed and pushed Apa on the shoulder. She said, That dog looks just like you. No wonder it followed you home. Then Mi Shi got to stay and be my friend. I like it when Apa is nice and Uhmma makes her squeaky-shoes laugh. Amen.

When I open my eyes Halmoni is looking at me sneaky peek.

That was a long prayer, she says and turns a page. What did you pray about?

That God would come down and give Apa a spanking, I tell her.

Halmoni holds her Good Book tight with both hands. She whispers, He is the only one who can.

Mi Gook

Mi Gook. This is a magic word. It can make Uhmma and Apa stop fighting like some important person is knocking on the door. Dirty brown boxes all tied up, with big black letters in the middle and little pictures all in the corner. They come from Mi Gook. Uhmma says they are from my Gomo. She is older than Apa. His big Uhn-nee. Inside the boxes there are funny toys for me. Like the one that plays tinkle-tinkle music and the scary man with rainbow paint on his face and hair jumping out.

Apa says that in Mi Gook everyone can make lots of money even if they did not go to an important school in the city. Uhmma says all the uhmmas in Mi Gook are pretty like dolls. And they live in big houses. Much bigger than the rich fish factory man's house in the village. Even Ju Mi, my friend who is one year older and likes to boss me around, says she would like to go to Mi Gook.

Then one day Apa gets a letter that makes him hug Uhmma so tight her eyes cry. Now every time Apa says Mi Gook, he smiles so big

I think maybe he is a doggy like Mi Shi. When we are eating our dinner, Apa and Uhmma can only say Mi Gook all the time. No more mean eyes over the rice bowl, and my stomach keeps the rice inside like a good stomach is supposed to do. I hope they will talk about Mi Gook forever and ever.

Mi Gook is the best word. Even better than sea or candy. But then when I go to Ju Mi's house to play with my new ball from Gomo, Ju Mi pushes me away.

She says, You are moving to Mi Gook and I feel so sorry for you because you have to leave everything behind.

I bounce my ball and think Ju Mi is talking, talking like she always does. Ju Mi takes the ball away and yells, Did you hear me? You are moving.

What? I yell at her and try to get my ball back.

Stupid. You are moving to Mi Gook.

No, I am not, I say, even though I do not know what moving means.

Stupid baby, she says. You do not even know you are moving away. Your uhmma told my uhmma today. I am happy you are moving so I do not have to play with a baby all the time.

I do not understand why Ju Mi says she is happy when her smile is sticking on her face upside down. I run away to find Uhmma.

Uhmma is outside in the yard squeezing laundry. I pull on her arm and say, Uhmma, Ju Mi says we are moving to Mi Gook.

Sit down, Uhmma says and sits back on her feet, butt close to the ground, knees sticking up to the sky.

I sit back on my legs next to her.

Young Ju, Uhmma says, you know we will be moving to Mi Gook soon.

No, I say. What is moving?

Your Apa and I have been talking about Mi Gook at dinner for days now.

Yes, Uhmma. But you never told me about moving. Does it mean we are going to see Gomo like when we went to see your uhmma and apa?

No. Moving is not like when we went to visit your Eh-Halmoni and Eh-Harabugi. Moving means we will live in Mi Gook for-ever.

Forever?

Yes.

Where is Mi Gook? Can I still come back to see Ju Mi?

Uhmma pets my hair. No, Young Ju. Mi Gook is far across the sea. We will have to take an airplane that flies in the sky to get there. I do not think you will be able to see Ju Mi for a long time. Uhmma stands up slowly.

Aigoo, she says as she always does when her legs hurt from sitting too long.

I keep sitting. I am thinking if I do not see Ju Mi every day then she will find a new friend. Someone who is not a baby. Maybe that new girl with brown pebble teeth. And what about my house? Who will take care of my small house that sits like a hen on her nest? Thinking about leaving Ju Mi and my house by the sea makes my heart hurt. Like someone is poking it with a stick. Ahya.

But then my eyes find the sky. Think about flying up, up, up. Now I know where we are going. I want to run around, wag my tail like Mi Shi. God is in the sky. Mi Gook must be in heaven and I have always wanted to go to heaven. It is just like the Good Book says. All people who love God will go to heaven someday. I love you, God, I whisper. In heaven you have to wear your Sunday dress every day so you can look pretty for God. Ju Mi must be mad because she wants to be me. Ju Mi likes to look pretty all the time and her uhmma lets her dress up only for church.

Uhmma hangs up the wet clothes. She sings soft and tickly as seagull feathers. My eyes are so wide I think maybe they will fall out. Uhmma never sings. Not even in church. She says singing takes too much heart and her heart is too heavy to give to God.

What are you singing, Uhmma?
Ah-me-ri-ka.
What is that?
Mi Gook.
This is a magic word.

Hair

Today Uhmma says I can wear my best dress. It has buttons shiny as the sun. Even though it has a small hole in the elbow from when Ju Mi pushed me down, Uhmma says, Wear it anyway because that is the only nice dress you have and try not to raise your arm too high.

I wait outside for Uhmma and pretend I do not see Mi Shi wagging her tail. I cannot get dirty. Uhmma said so. Then Mi Shi rolls on her back.

See my stomach, she barks.

Maybe just one pet, I say.

Mi Shi licks my hand.

Uhmma slides back the door. Why are you playing with Mi Shi when I told you not to get dirty? she says. Come on. We are going to be late.

Uhmma is wearing her fancy going-out dress. Her long hair plays in the wind. Almost all the time Uhmma twists her hair tight as wet laundry and sticks it on top of her head like on the Buddha statues in the park. But today is not a workday. Today we are going to

19

an important place to make me pretty for Mi Gook.

I do not like to be pretty. Pretty means you cannot play in your nice clothes and Uhmma grabs your hair with a wet comb until your eyes are pulled shut and then she ties it all up with a bow and says, You look very pretty. Uhmma says that sometimes I have to look pretty so everyone will see what a nice girl I can be.

Uhmma pulls my hand and I walk fast so she will not get mad and thump my head like a ripe watermelon. I watch Uhmma's shoes talk to the road.

Dok dok dok.

Shiny, nighttime-sky shoes.

Dok dok dok.

I can walk on my tiptoes too.

Dok dok curls.

Curls? Uhmma, what did you say? I ask.

Aigoo, Young Ju! I told you to listen to me closely. You are always dreaming when you should be listening. An ahjimma will curl your hair so you will look just like a real Mi Gook girl.

Curls? What are they? I ask. Show me, Uhmma.

Curls, Uhmma says. Like this. She points in the air and goes round and round. She looks in my eyes. She says, Think about the waves in the sea.

I nod.

Remember how the water rises up as if it is looking for the land and then it falls back around to join the sea when it comes close to the beach? That is a circle. Those are curls.

Uhmma, there will be curls in my hair? I ask and hold up some of my hair.

Yes, Is that not exciting? Gomo says lots of Mi Gook people have curly hair. Gomo even has curly hair now.

Uhmma, are you going to have curls? I ask.

Uhmma laughs at my question. Today she does not bite her lip and open her nose holes big as fish mouths and say, Too many questions. Enough.

Uhmma picks me up, holds me tight. I am too old to change, she says.

I play with Uhmma's long black hair. Wrap it around my fingers.

But listen now, Young Ju.

I play with Uhmma's hair and think, Someday I will have hair that is stronger than rope.

In Mi Gook, you can grow up to be anything you want.

I will have hair that can play in the wind light as a kite. And feel softer than my first-birthday silk jacket.

You, little one, are my hope.

I hold Uhmma's hair and shut my eyes tight. Pray real fast like I do at night. Please,

God, heavenly Father, please do not give me curly hair.

Uhmma pinches my nose and laughs, Why is your face wrinkled up like an old halmoni?

Outside the important place that will make me pretty, Uhmma fixes the bow in my hair. She tucks my hair behind my ears. Good, she says and then opens the door. We step inside. My nose wrinkles iee! This cannot be the special place. There are ugly smells inside. Worse than Halmoni boiling clothes in soapy water. Uhmma sees my nose and gives me the squinty eye. I push my nose back down.

An ahjimma comes out from behind a curtain and greets Uhmma in a loud voice. When she bends over to bow I see her picking food out of her teeth with her tongue. Uhmma bows and then pushes me forward so I can show her my good manners. I try not to wrinkle my nose at the ahjimma when I say, Ahn-young-ha-say-yo, and give her a deep bow. The ahjimma pats my head and says I am a good girl for walking such a long way.

We are here for the curly-hair treatment, Uhmma says.

Yes. Your husband said you would be stopping in. Please sit down. I will get my equipment.

When the ahjimma goes behind the curtain, I pull Uhmma's hand. I like my straight hair, I tell her. I am too old to change. I do not want to be a Mi Gook girl. Let us go before the ahjimma comes back.

Uhmma bites her bottom lip and her nose holes open big. Young Ju, why are you talking such nonsense? Uhmma says. We are going to Mi Gook so you can have the very best education. So someday you will be better than a fisherman's wife. Uhmma holds out her hands. Look at my rough hands. Do you think I always had hands like these? Do you want to end up like this? Uhmma touches my cheek with her cat-tongue fingers and says, Your Apa thought you were too young to have such an expensive hairstyle, but I told him you were old enough now. You can understand how important it is to look like a real Mi Gook girl. Young Ju, are you a big girl who understands?

No, I cry. No curly hair.

Uhmma grabs my shoulders. What is wrong with you? Be quiet. Here comes the ahjimma.

I do not want curly hair, I say. No. No. No.

Uhmma raises her hand. Open. Flat as a paddle. Young Ju, Uhmma growls.

No, Uhmma.

Young Ju.

I hold my breath.

Uhmma keeps her hand in the air. Young

Ju, are you going to be a good girl?

I swallow. Yes.

Uhmma pats her cheek the way she does when she is worried and tells the ahjimma, I am so embarrassed. Please accept my apology for my spoiled daughter.

No need to apologize, the ahjimma says. Children can be very difficult these days. Young Ju, come sit over here.

I stare at the floor and walk over to the red chair. I sit down. The ahjimma pulls out my bow. My hair falls around my face. It tickles my cheeks. I close my eyes.

Making curly hair takes a long time. The ahjimma and Uhmma talk about Mi Gook the whole time. Comb some hair. Mi Gook. Pull. Twist. Mi Gook. Pour on stinky laundry water. Mi Gook. My stomach wants to push out all the morning rice.

The ahjimma washes my hair and dries it with a towel. She pokes her fingers all over my head. There, she says. Stand up now. You can open your eyes. We are done. Your hair looks very pretty.

I stand up, but I do not open my eyes. I am afraid. My hair is tickling my ears now. Not my cheeks.

Young Ju, come here, Uhmma says.

I tell my feet to go, but they are stuck to the floor. I open my eyes and make my feet run to

Uhmma's leg. I hide my face in Uhmma's dress. Smells good. Like when Apa took us to see mountain trees smaller than me. Uhmma's hands touch my hair.

Young Ju, Uhmma says, look in the mirror. Look at all your pretty curls. Uhmma holds my shoulders and turns me around.

Who is that girl? She cannot be me. Her hair is too big. It stands up big as a bush, just like the hair of the toy man with the rainbow face. Uhmma did not tell me this was curly hair. She said it would look like the sea. But it does not. I am a Mi Gook girl with big ugly toy-man hair.

Do you like it, Young Ju? Uhmma is smiling. Happy lots of teeth smile. Happy as the letter about Mi Gook. Happy at me. Even though Uhmma tells me I should always tell the truth, and Halmoni says God will be very angry if you lie, I want Uhmma to smile happy lots of teeth at me.

Young Ju, do you like your curly hair?

I look at the floor. Yes, I lie, quiet as snow.

Waiting for Heaven

I do not like this bus that bounces and rolls like a boat on stormy waters. I pull on Uhmma's shirt. When will this bus get to Mi Gook? I ask.

This is not a bus, Apa answers. It is an airplane. Go to sleep and stop bothering your Uhmma. We will tell you when we are there.

I play with the bow on my new going-to-Mi-Gook dress so I do not have to look at Apa's eyes. He might get mad. I pat the skirt over my knees. Feels better than bunny rabbit fur. It is the color of the nighttime sky just before the sun goes down. Halmoni's quiet time, time for a walk and talk about olden days. Halmoni said, This dress will remind you of me. It will help you remember our walks.

I pat my dress and wish this dress were Halmoni. Thinking about Halmoni all alone in our sitting-hen house makes me want to cry louder than Ju Mi's baby sister who has no hair.

Mi Gook is only for young people to have a new start, Halmoni said. Not for old people who are used-up dry fish bones.

I do not understand why Mi Gook is only for Apa and Uhmma and me. God said everyone could go to heaven. Maybe God is a big liar. If Halmoni cannot go to Mi Gook, then I do not want to go. I want to stay at home with Halmoni.

The bus jumps one big jump. *Kunk!* God is angry I called him a liar. He knows I do not want to go to Mi Gook! I close my eyes tight and pray, Dear Father who lives in heaven. I am sorry. I do want to see all the pretty angels who wear white dresses and fly in the air. I do want to see Harabugi.

Kunk! I open my eyes, grab Uhmma's shirt. I try to crawl into her lap. I cannot. There is thick rope holding me down.

Uhmma. Uhmma. Help, I say.

Uhmma opens one eye, then the other eye. What is wrong? she says. Why are you not sleeping?

God is angry that I do not want to go to Mi Gook without Halmoni, I say.

Shhh, that is foolish talk. God is not angry. Sleep now. I will sing you a song.

Uhmma. Can everyone go to heaven?

Yes. If they are God's people.

Is Halmoni God's people?

Halmoni is the one who first heard God's words from Pastor Shin.

Then Halmoni can go to heaven?

Yes, Young Ju. She will be there one day. Now, close your eyes. If you sleep, we will get to Mi Gook faster.

I smile. Halmoni is coming to Mi Gook! It is not just for young people. I close my eyes and Uhmma sings the mountain rabbit song. This is my song, only Halmoni was the one who would rub my back and sing it to me so I could fall asleep.

San toki. Toki ya.

Uhmma?

Young Ju, no more questions.

Please, Uhmma, one more. Do you think Halmoni is sleeping too?

Yes, she is. Do not worry about Halmoni. She can take care of herself. She will miss you, but she knows Mi Gook is best for you. It is time to sleep. Halmoni is probably waiting for you in your dreams.

Uhmma puts her arm over my shoulder. I close my eyes and try to dream. I do not want Halmoni to wait long. She is old and her back gets tired. I let Uhmma sing the song.

San toki. Toki ya. Uh dee ru ga nun yah. Ghang choung. Ghang choung dee men su. Uh dee ru ga nun yah.

I am a mountain rabbit bouncing, running. Where am I going? I am going to see Harabugi. And when Halmoni comes, I will ask her if she liked the bus that is called an airplane. In Mi Gook, everyone will be happy and filled with love. I am a mountain rabbit bouncing, running, closing my eyes. Waiting for heaven.

A Step from Heaven

I am looking for Harabugi all over Gomo's house. There are so many rooms. All of the floors are covered with a warm white blanket that is soft on my feet. And the rooms do not have rice paper doors but a big piece of wood like the stores in the village. Everyone in heaven must be very rich to have so many blankets and wooden doors inside the house.

Young Ju, where are you? Uhmma calls. I try to find her voice, but I am lost. When I open a door, there is only another room. Sometimes small. Sometimes big. This room has a funny seat with pink fur on it. Soft. I wonder what kind of animal in Mi Gook has pink fur.

I sit on the fur seat. There is a fat ball of snowy paper stuck on the wall. When I pull on the end, it rolls out like a long tail of smoke.

Young Ju, what are you doing? Everyone is waiting for you in the big room, Uhmma says from the doorway.

I jump off the seat and run to Uhmma. She picks me up and carries me away.

In the big room, Apa is sitting next to Sahmchun, who is a Mi Gook person with big round money eyes like in the picture of God. Only his money eyes are not dark as night. They are daytime, sun-is-shining, sky-color eyes. His hair is wavy brown seaweed. He says to call him Uhing Kel Thim. That is Mi Gook talk for Sahmchun, but my mouth does not want to make those words. He says it is fine to call him Sahmchun until my mouth is ready to learn.

He is sitting and talking with Apa and Gomo. He makes our words with a big floppy tongue.

Here she is, Uhmma says and bounces me in her arms.

Give her to me. I will hold her, Sahmchun says.

Uhmma puts me down on Sahmchun's lap. I want to touch Sahmchun's sky eyes. But that is not nice. Poor Sahmchun. He will think I am making fun of his eyes like when I got curly hair and Ju Mi was laughing, laughing so much she could not talk.

Do you like the house, Young Ju? Sahmchun asks.

It is very big and nice. But I did not find Harabugi. Where is he? I ask.

Sahmchun's eyebrows wrinkle together. Harabugi? He asks, Why does Harabugi live here?

Everyone at the table is looking at me.

Young Ju, that is a stupid question, Apa says. Harabugi is in heaven.

This is heaven, I say. Mi Gook is heaven. Where is Harabugi?

Now they are all shaking their heads. Apa gives me hard rock eyes. Sahmchun rubs his chin.

Young Ju, Sahmchun says. Mi Gook is not heaven. Harabugi is with God.

We are not in the sky with God?

He shakes his head.

I ask, Then how do you have all the blankets on the floor and big wooden doors? Everyone in heaven is rich and happy.

Sahmchun shakes his head again. He says, Mi Gook is very nice. But it is not heaven.

My eyes turn down. My lips turn down. Sahmchun watches my face. He bounces me on his knees and holds up one finger. Wait, he says. Mi Gook is almost as good as heaven. Let us say it is a step from heaven.

I do not like his words. A step from heaven? I crawl off his lap and stand up straight. I say loud in my best voice, If this is not heaven, I want to go home. Halmoni is waiting for me.

Young Ju, Apa says. Sit down. I do not want to hear any more nonsense from you. Apa stands up and grabs the back of my dress.

He pulls me to a chair next to him and makes me sit.

I will not cry. No. I hold my breath.

Uhmma is making a sound that is not her squeaky-shoes laugh. More like dragging a stick on the ground. Uhmma pats her cheek and says, Young Ju has such an imagination. She is always dreaming when she should be listening.

Gomo rubs my back. She says, What a funny girl you are, Young Ju. Where did you get the idea that Mi Gook was heaven? Halmoni must have filled your head with too many stories. Well, you are here now and you can become a Mi Gook girl. Here, try this drink. Everyone in Mi Gook loves Ko-ka Ko-la. They drink it like water. You will love it too.

Gomo gives me a cup with dirty black water inside. I can see bubbles floating. Maybe this is a drink from the sea. I sniff the cup like Mi Shi.

Just drink it, Young Ju, Apa growls.

I put the cup to my mouth and take a small taste. Ahya! It hurts. This drink bites the inside of my mouth and throat like swallowing tiny fish bones. This is what Mi Gook people love? I want to push the drink away, but I cannot show bad manners.

Good girl, Young Ju. Drink that up and you

can have more, Apa says. He pats my head.

I hold the cup in my hands. Uhmma and Apa talk to Sahmchun and Gomo. They do not see my wet eyes and hurting mouth. They are happy to be in Mi Gook. Many jobs, big houses, good schools, make a living, they say back and forth. Uhmma sits close to Apa. Their shoulders touch. Uhmma smiles at Apa. Apa smiles back.

I do not understand why they are showing happy teeth. Do they not miss Halmoni? Are they not mad that they are not in the real heaven? Harabugi is waiting in the real heaven and Halmoni will go there without me. I do not care if we are a step from heaven. I take a big swallow of the hurting drink. This is not heaven.

My Future

I do not like the word school. Uhmma and Apa say school is my future. I do not like the word future. Everything is in the future. A house we do not have to share with Gomo and Sahmchun. A car without big cuts in the seat that show the crumbly insides that Uhmma says I should not pull out, but I do anyway because it feels like sand when you mush it between your fingers.

Only now when I sit in the back seat I have to cover the parts that say a little mouse has been here because I am the only Mouse in the family. Everyone else has important signs like Tiger or Dragon. The new baby that is still waiting inside Uhmma's stomach will be born in the Year of the Dragon. But that is in the future.

I think future must mean a long time away. Except school is not in the future. It is now. I do not understand how school is my future when it is not a long time away. I will have to ask the teacher. Apa says the teacher will know everything and I should listen hard because then I have to teach him and

Uhmma what I learned.

Inside school everyone is running and playing with toys. A tall ahjimma, even taller than Apa, comes over. She has a big white cloud sitting on top of her head like it is hair. Apa bows just when the lady puts out her hand and he hits it with his forehead. She laughs. Apa shakes his head. Then he holds her hand and lets it drop. He pushes me forward and says, Greet your teacher, Young Ju.

The lady with the cloud hair is my teacher? But she is a giant person like in the long-ago stories Halmoni used to tell me so I would be a good girl. My teacher looks like the old witch who ate bad children for dinner.

Apa taps my head and says loud, Young. The witch teacher says, "Ho ha do, Yung."

I pull on Apa's shirt and say, Apa. My name is not Young. It is Young Ju. You forgot the Ju part.

Shhh, Young Ju, Apa says, in school you are only Young. Mi Gook people will have too much trouble saying all the syllables. It is better to keep it simple for them. Now, bow to your teacher.

Ahn-young-ha-say-yo, I say and bow so I can show her good manners and she will not eat me up.

Apa puts two round monies in my hand. This is for food, he says. Obey the teacher,

Young Ju, and listen well. Gomo will be here to pick you up after school. Apa waves to me and then leaves for his gardening job.

"Ah ri cas, ca mo ve he," the witch teacher says. She claps her hands and then touches her cloud hair. All the other Mi Gook girls and boys come over fast like they are scared they will be eaten if they are not good children. They sit in a circle around me.

"Tees es Yung," the witch teacher says.

"Wah ko um, Yung," they say.

I see some girls whispering to each other. I have never seen so many different colors of hair. Some are shiny brown like mud in the rain. One boy and one girl have hair the color of wheat waving in the sun. I wonder if it crackles when their uhmma brushes it. I count, hana, duool, seht, neht. Neht have night hair like me. But not all the Americans have curly hair like Gomo said they would. Only one boy has big curly hair. I hope they do not think I am a boy.

I am looking at all the hair, but then the witch teacher says more Mi Gook words and everyone runs to sit down at the tables. The teacher holds my hand and takes me to a chair next to a girl with night hair. Her shirt is the color of the sea. I want to touch her shirt, but I am scared.

"Hee," she says and holds out a red stick. I

shake my head because I do not know how to talk Mi Gook. Sea Shirt rubs the red stick on some paper and the color stays there. There are many color sticks inside the box and Sea Shirt is pulling them out and rubbing them on the paper. Sea Shirt stops rubbing the sticks and watches me chew on my finger. She holds out the red stick again. This time I know what to do.

I am rubbing the color sticks on the paper for a long time. I make a sea and sand. Then in the corner I draw our sitting-hen house. There is so much to fill in that I do not hear the witch teacher talking. All the girls and boys run outside. I am the only one sitting down with my color sticks. The witch teacher is talking, talking, fast like she is mad. I cover my ears. I am so scared I feel like I have to go to the bathroom. I have disobeyed and the witch teacher will eat me.

The witch teacher sits down next to me and scratches her head. Her finger disappears into the cloud. Up close the witch teacher does not look so mean. The small chair makes her knees almost touch her chin. I smile. When the witch teacher smiles back I think maybe she will not eat me.

The teacher takes my hands away from my ears. "Yung," she says.

I shake my head. The teacher pats her

cloud hair and then looks around. She walks over to the corner of the room and comes back with a bowl. She sits back down and takes something out of the bowl and puts it in her mouth. Her mouth moves up and down, up and down. Her head goes back and forth, back and forth. Mi Gook teachers eat very funny. I lean over to see what is inside the bowl. There is nothing there. Maybe the teacher is playing.

The teacher points to her lips and says, "Laanchu." Then she is eating from the empty bowl again.

I say, "Laanchu," and chew hard like I am eating a piece of dried squid. This makes the teacher so happy she is clapping and smiling and saying, "Goo, goo!"

The teacher watches me. Again I say the word that makes her so happy, "Laanchu." But this time the teacher does not clap. She twists her lip in the corner.

I say, "Laanchu."

The teacher holds her chin. I play with my color sticks and pretend I do not see her thinking about eating me. After a very long time, the teacher gets up and goes to her desk. She comes back with a bag filled with big yellow crumbs. They are just like the car seat crumbs I am not supposed to pick at. I am worried. The teacher knows I disobeyed Uhmma.

The teacher takes one of the crumbs, puts it in her mouth. She sits down and holds out the bag. I pull out a crumb. The big yellow crumb up close looks like something I know. I turn it around and around until I see the little tail. It reminds me of the little fishes Uhmma dries for dinner. I make the little fish swim in the air. The teacher nods. "Yehs!" she says.

"Yehs," I say and make the fish swim more. "Yehs."

"Noo," the teacher says, shaking her head. She points to the fish. "Go-do-feesh."

I point to the fish. "Go-do-feesh?"

"Yehs," the teacher says, nodding. "Go-do-feesh."

Then the teacher pours a big pile of Go-do-feesh onto my picture of the sea and gets up. Her tall legs push her high into the air. I am afraid her head will hit the roof. She looks down at me and puts another Go-do-feesh into her mouth. She chews and says, "Laanchu." She points to me.

I put one Go-do-feesh in my mouth and bite it slowly. It crunches like sand. A smoky salty taste sits on my tongue. These Go-do-feesh are good to eat. I nod and say, "Laanchu." The teacher smiles and goes to sit behind her desk.

I make the Go-do-feesh swim in the sea and then get eaten by a big sea monster. When the girls and boys come back inside, the big sea monster has eaten all the Go-do-feesh. This bad sea monster has forgotten to save one to teach Uhmma and Apa. I am so sad my head is hanging sideways on my neck. I will get a big thump from Uhmma's knuckle. Then I remember that I have the rubbing sticks. I draw the Go-do-feesh into my sea.

Sea Shirt points to my picture and says, "Go-do-feesh."

I say, "Laanchu."

Sea Shirt talks fast Mi Gook words.

I shake my head. Smile. I know only little Mi Gook words now. But someday I will know all of them. In the future.

Not Forever

It is not forever, Apa says to Uhmma. They sit in the front of the car, looking out at the house. Old brown paint peeling off. Old brown grass flying away. Crisscross metal fence all around. Apa pushes in the magic light button for his cigarette. Uhmma rubs her blow-up stomach. Round and round. I am afraid Uhmma will pop like the balloons at my first Mi Gook birthday party.

Apa turns in his seat and says to me, This will not really be our house. We will just borrow the bottom part from the man who lives upstairs.

Uhmma turns to Apa. Could we not wait longer and save more money?

Apa lights his cigarette. Blows out the smoke. He shakes his head. You know what it is like. How can you stand to live like that? Always thanking them, always having to be careful. We have no privacy.

Yes, you are right. But soon the baby will be here and then I can work. I will look for two jobs and then we can save for our own house.

Woman, what are you talking about? Apa

rolls down the window and sticks his cigarette outside. Tap, tap.

I just mean the baby is only a few weeks away. I can work soon. Could you not wait a few more months?

What did I just tell you! Apa shouts. Woman, were you listening? Did you hear anything I said? I do not want to grovel anymore like some bitch. What is saving more money going to do? What? Get you a fancy house? Is that what you want? I cannot provide you with enough?

No, I do not mean that, Uhmma says quietly. She keeps her hands on her stomach. Round and round.

Tap, tap. Apa puts the cigarette in his mouth. Takes a sip and then blows out smoke. He faces out to the house and growls, You always want more. Better.

Apa's voice changes. Write to your sister, he says in a squeaky-mouse voice. Let us move to Mi Gook. We will have a better life.

Apa turns and faces Uhmma. He points to her stomach. Look at us now. This is all your fault. You hear me? Your fault I had to take a second job picking up those lawyers' trash like some beggar. In Korea at least I had my own boat. What was so bad about that life?

Yuhboh, Yuhboh, Uhmma says. She uses her special husband word to make him stop.

Try to make him be nice. I crawl up into the corner of the back seat. I keep my eyes on Uhmma's perfect half-moon face.

I told you it is not forever, Apa says. Smoke fills the car and then floats away with the wind.

Yuhboh, I understand, Uhmma says. You must do what is best.

Apa leans his arm on the car door, his elbow sticking out the window. He says quietly, We will pay rent for now and try to save slowly for our own house.

Uhmma rolls down her window and sighs.

Apa's head, snap, turns to her. Yah, he says. What are you sighing about? What? I told you it is not forever.

Uhmma keeps her face looking out the window. Rubs her stomach. Round and round. She does not answer.

Apa sticks his cigarette out the window. Tap, tap. He says again, We will save slowly.

But, Uhmma says to her stomach and then stops. She reaches up and pats her cheek with one hand. Uhmma starts again, If we stayed with Gomo we could save more quickly. If I worked two jobs and we did not have to pay rent, we could save enough money for a down payment in no time.

I do not see Apa's hand. It is too fast. I only hear the slap, loud as breaking glass.

I bite my bottom lip. Hard. I cannot cry. It will only make it worse. I close my eyes and start to pray, Please, God, please make everything better.

What did I say, Apa yells. Slap.

I open my eyes and look at Uhmma. She covers her lip with her hand. A little blood comes out from between her fingers. My tears are falling onto my knees. I hold my breath so I will not cry out. Say letters in my head, A B C D E F G.

What did I say? Apa asks Uhmma.

Uhmma looks straight at the house, her hand covering her lip. She does not answer. Apa leans close to Uhmma. Face to face. His eyes squint thin as paper. He takes the used-up cigarette from his lips and holds it between his thumb and finger.

Please, Uhmma, I say in my head. Please say it. Please. Please. Please.

Uhmma takes away her hand. Blood drips down her chin. Her lips are broken grapes. She says with her eyes closed, It is not forever.

Park Joon Ho

Gomo said she would play with me when she came over to our new house that is not really our house, just the one we are borrowing for now, but Gomo only wants to look at baby things. Gomo holds all the baby things in her hands and sits down on the yellow blanket that covers the couch. I peek and make sure the blanket did not get messed up. Uhmma said it is my job to make sure the blanket always covers the cushions so no one will see the burn holes the old owner made.

I sit on the couch next to Gomo and kick out my feet. I am tired of waiting. I am tired of naps in the afternoon because it is too hot to play outside. I wish school would start so I can be in the second grade. In the second grade, you can buy your lunch if you bring money to school. John Chuchurelli told me. He knows because he has a big sister in third grade. I kick out my feet and stare at the white bows on my shoes. I want to rip them off, stupid baby feet, but Uhmma said Gomo would be sad if I messed up the special birthday shoes that Gomo and Uncle Tim picked out just for me. Where are Apa and Uncle Tim? They said they would be back soon with Uhmma and the new baby.

Gomo picks up a blue shirt and holds it up. Young Ju, Gomo says and turns to me. Did you know that when you were born you had a blue spot right above your little butt? Gomo leans forward and points behind her back at the spot.

No, I did not know, Gomo, I say and kick out my feet again. Stupid baby bows.

Gomo keeps talking. She says, Naturally, you do not have the spot now. It disappears as you get older. But when you were first born, it was there. Every Han Gook baby has that spot. It is the mark of our blood. Our heritage. A long, long time ago, all Han Gook people came from Mongolia.

If I did not have the bows, my shoes would look just like the ones the dancers have on TV.

Did you know, Young Ju, Gomo says and folds the baby shirt in a square, Genghis Khan —

Outside, a car door slams. Gomo and I turn to the door. They are here. I jump off the couch and run to the front door. Apa opens the door and walks inside, carefully holding a blanket. I stand on my toes to see what is in the blanket, but Apa is too tall. Uhmma comes from behind me and pats my head.

Young Ju, were you a good girl while I was away? Uhmma asks. Her eyes are sleepy and there is no more balloon stomach. I jump up and try to make her pick me up.

Apa calls out, Young Ju, do not worry your Uhmma. She is too tired to carry you. Besides, you are not a baby anymore.

Uncle Tim comes inside with a bag in each of his hands. He puts one bag by the couch and then takes the other bag to Uhmma.

What is this? Uhmma asks.

A surprise, Uncle Tim says. Here, sit down and open it.

Before Uhmma sits down, she calls out to Apa, Let Young Ju look at the baby.

Apa nods and then bends down. Look, Young Ju, Apa says. This is your new brother, Park Joon Ho. Is he not beautiful?

Inside there is a wiggly worm with no hair. I touch his head and feel only a little fur. I ask Apa, Where is his hair?

It will grow in later, Apa says.

I look back at the worm. Maybe his hair will be curly because he was born in Mi Gook.

Uhmma is calling out to Uncle Tim, "Tank uh, Theem." Uhmma holds a big bottle in her hands.

Champagne is for a celebration, Uncle Tim says. For important times.

Apa says, Yes, there is much to celebrate. "Tank you, Tim."

Gomo walks over to Apa and says, Let me hold the baby now.

Apa gives her the blanket with the worm. Gomo makes animal noises. Cluck cluck like a chicken. Woo woo like an owl. Apa stands next to Gomo and makes his finger into a baby snake saying hello. The snake tickles the worm's head.

Look, Apa says, pointing. Look at my son yawning. Only one day old and he yawns with the concentration of a wise man.

Uhmma stands up and walks over to the other side of Gomo. She puts her face close to the worm. Closes her eyes and takes a deep breath. Uhmma looks up at Apa and says, Someday he could be a doctor or a lawyer.

Gomo adds, Someday he could be president.

Apa's eyes find the window by the front door. They stare past the old brown grass, past the crisscross metal fence. They travel far, far away. Someday, Apa says, my son will make me proud.

I can be president, Apa, I call out.

Apa's eyes are back home. Pointing at me. He laughs. You are a girl, Young Ju.

Yuhboh, Uhmma says. Leave her to dream. Do not be so harsh.

Uncle Tim picks me up. "Young Ju," he whispers into my hair, "in America, women can do almost anything men can do."

His words do not make the hurt in my heart go away. The cut of Apa's laugh is still open. Uncle Tim bounces me in his arms. Look, he says to Apa and Uhmma. Two beautiful children.

One of the beautiful children, Uhmma says, needs to be changed. Uhmma picks up the bag by the couch and takes out a white square.

I will change him, Apa says and takes the worm from Gomo.

Uhmma's eyes open wide. She asks, Do you know how to do it?

I can learn, Apa says.

Uhmma laughs and turns to Gomo. With Young Ju, Uhmma says, he could not even hold her.

Everyone laughs. I stare down at my bows. Apa did not even want to hold me.

Am I doing this right? Apa calls out from the couch.

I will get some glasses for the champagne, Uncle Tim says. Wait here.

Go help him, Apa tells Uhmma.

Uhmma hurries after Uncle Tim to the kitchen. Gomo and Apa are busy with the worm.

I wander over to the couch and start to tuck in the corners of the yellow blanket. Gomo says, What a good housekeeper you are. Here, sit down and watch what we are doing. You will have to learn how to be a good older Uhn-nee. It is your responsibility to help your Uhmma take care of him.

I stand next to Gomo. The worm's eyes are shut tight. Why does he get to be president? I am the one who is stronger and bigger.

Apa takes off the diaper. My nose wrinkles iee! This worm stinks. Apa laughs. He even smells like me, Apa says.

I turn my head away. Did I smell like Apa when I was a baby? Why did Apa not hold me? Then I remember Gomo's words. All Han Gook babies have a blue spot. I had a blue spot. Maybe this worm does not have a blue spot because he was born in Mi Gook. Maybe he cannot be a real Park and I will be the only one who can make Apa proud. I lean over Gomo's shoulder to watch Apa change the worm.

Most times Apa's hands are dark and hard with dirt from his gardening job. Other times they are rough and peeling from his cleaning job. Today Apa's hands are soft and clean. Praying hands. For the baby. Apa carefully lifts the baby's legs and cleans his bottom. I check for the spot. There, in the place Gomo said it would be, is the blue. Faint as an old bruise. The baby opens his eyes and looks right at me.

Apa finishes with the diaper just as Uncle Tim and Uhmma come out of the kitchen with glasses. Uncle Tim calls out and waves everyone over to him like he is starting Sharing Circle.

Here, Young Ju, Gomo says. Make sure the baby does not roll off the couch. Stand here so you can protect him. Gomo moves me in front of the baby. I stand straight as a door.

Behind me, there is a loud *pong!* I turn my head and see Uncle Tim holding the big bottle with white sea foam spilling out. Apa, Uhmma, and Gomo hold out their glasses.

A toast, Uncle Tim says, raising his glass. A toast for the new baby.

To my son, Park Joon Ho, Apa calls out.

Park Joon Ho, everyone cheers.

I reach down and pull a bow off my shoe. I am not a baby anymore.

Burying Lies

In second grade you have to do a lot of talking. Not as much coloring. Not as much play time. Just a lot of talking and listening and reading. So in Mrs. Sheldon's class, if you do not have anything to show when it is your turn to share, you can talk about important news. I have nothing to show, but I want to say something important. Something I have been thinking about for a long time.

Finally, when it is my turn to share, I run up to the front of the classroom. I put my hands behind my back, cross my fingers, and tell everyone, "My brother. He die."

"Oh, my. Oh, I'm sorry," Mrs. Sheldon says, then hurries over to hug me. She pulls me close. So close I can smell the sour-blossom stink under her arms and her long brown hair tickles my face. I pull away and look up at her.

"I the only Park now. I keep name like boy."

Her forehead bunches up like crinkled paper and her eyes squeeze shut in the corners. She does not understand the English that sounds perfect in my head and then comes out messy as the can of spaghetti Uhmma lets me eat on Saturdays if I help with the laundry.

John Chuchurelli, who always has to sit on the Time-Out rug, raises his hand and asks, "How did he die?"

"John," Mrs. Sheldon shouts, "what a thing to ask! Do you want to sit on the rug?"

John looks like he is thinking maybe this is a good idea. The rug is far from the blackboard and that means he does not have to pay attention. But then he shakes his head no. Mrs. Sheldon blows out her breath. I run back to my desk while Mrs. Sheldon stands in front of the class plucking at the skin of her neck. She always does that when she is thinking.

"You know what, class? I know it's not a Friday, but I think this is a good time to make Young a warm fuzzy. Don't you think that will make Young and her family feel better?"

"Yes!" everybody cheers because warm fuzzies are only for Fridays after the spelling test and today is Wednesday. Warm fuzzies take half a day to make and half a day to clean up. Yarn puddles all over the floor until all that is left are a few round, fuzzy balls with strange names like Pluto, Strawberry, and Bluebeard.

For the whole morning everyone makes fuzzies. Then one by one they bring their fuzzies over to my desk. They put the fuzzy down and tell me its name.

"Please take care of Sunshine."

"I hope Melonhead makes you feel better."

Soon I have a million fuzzies covering my desk. I circle them with my arms and rub my cheeks against their soft yarn fur.

For silent reading Mrs. Sheldon lets me be the first to pick out a book. I get the one with all the pictures of Laura and Mary in the Big Woods. When I grow up I want to be a pioneer girl and help Ma make Christmas pies. At lunch, Amanda says I can have her last Lifesaver because her grandma died last year and she knows what it is like to be sad. I eat the Lifesaver, but it turns sour on my tongue. I spit it out when Amanda turns around to yell at John Chuchurelli, who is making kissing noises behind her back. After P.E., Mrs. Sheldon gives me a special card with lots of the scratch-and-sniff stickers she hands out only for perfect papers in spelling. My spelling is never perfect. But today I am special. I play with my fuzzies, scratch and sniff my stickers, and think about how nice it is that my brother is dead.

When I get home from school, Gomo, who comes over to watch us during the day so Uhmma can sew clothes at the factory, is playing with Joon Ho. She tickles his chin until he laughs so hard he throws up some milk. If I throw up milk I get a head thump from Uhmma. But since it is Joon Ho, great first son, he only gets kisses for messing up the carpet. Gomo stands up for a towel and then points to the kitchen table.

Young Ju, look at those pretty flowers. Your school sent them, Gomo says.

My eyes blink twice. Hard. Like they cannot believe those white and yellow flowers are sitting on the table. I take off my shoes and try to walk to my room.

Come here, Gomo says. She goes over to the flowers. I am so scared my toes curl into the carpet.

What does this mean? Gomo asks, waving a small white card. Why are they sorry about our loss? Even though Gomo has been here for a long time, her English is not that good.

I look down at the orange carpet and stare at all the shaggy strands between my toes. Think. Think. I look up at Gomo and something flies out of my mouth. "I loss spelling contest my school. I come in second."

Speak Korean, Gomo says. She likes to talk Korean at our house because in her house Uncle Tim wants only English. He wants Gomo to learn how to talk nice to his family. Gomo says speaking English all the time makes her head hurt.

I lost the spelling contest at school. I came in second, I say.

Second place. That is good news, not a loss. Your Uhmma and Apa will be so happy. Flowers for second place are very nice, Gomo says.

I hold my book bag with all the fuzzies and the special Mrs. Sheldon card close to my stomach and slowly back up toward the door. My feet feel around for my shoes. When I find them, I yell out to Gomo, I am going outside to play.

I do not want to answer any more questions. I have to hide the fuzzies and the card or else I will be in big trouble for lying.

Along the side of the house, where Mr. Owner keeps all the broken things like smashed windows and a tired chair with a missing seat, there is an old tree stump. The dirt around the stump is soft and crumbly. I pick up a stick and start to dig. Both hands work fast. Both ears listen for any Gomo footsteps. Soon a hole the size of a small pot grows down. I make sure no one is watching and open my school bag. I kiss each fuzzy goodbye.

"Sorry, Roly-Poly. Bye, Melonhead," I say and drop them into the hole. I sniff Mrs. Sheldon's pretty card with all the rainbow smells one more time and pat it down next to the fuzzies. I cover my lies with dirt.

I am in the bathroom washing my face and hands with soap three times when Uhmma gets home. Uhmma always says lies smell worse than dead fish. I can hear Gomo telling her about the flowers. I walk out of the bathroom. Uhmma stands by the kitchen table sniffing the flowers. Her eyes are closed.

Young Ju, come here, Gomo says, waving me to hurry up. I walk over to the couch and wonder if Uhmma can smell the lie in the flowers. Uhmma opens her eyes and holds out her arm for me. I take baby steps. Stop far away so she cannot smell me. But then Uhmma reaches out and pulls me close to her side. Her nose sinks into my hair, sniffing my head like Mi Shi used to do. I close my eyes and pray fast, Our Father who lives in heaven, I know I have not prayed every day like I am supposed to, but do not let Uhmma know about the lie and I will pray every night. I promise.

I am proud of you, Young Ju, Uhmma says, looking down into my eyes. You are a smart girl and someday you will be a smart woman. You just keep studying hard. I am going to put a flower in my prayer book. Uhmma picks out a perfect snowy blossom and snaps it off with her fingernail.

After Gomo leaves, Uhmma does not sit

too tired to talk on the couch with Joon Ho sleeping in her arms. Tonight she makes me sit next to her and talk about what I would like to be someday. Maybe I can be a doctor or a lawyer, or maybe a professor like some other important Parks. Uhmma tells me stories about the great Parks of our past while Joon Ho sleeps. I listen to Uhmma and think, I cannot be the great son, but I can do important things. Then I will be the famous Park in the family. Maybe even better than first son.

Even though I am supposed to be sleeping, my eyes are still open when Apa comes home from his night job cleaning the lawyers' offices. From my bed I can only hear Uhmma and Apa murr, murr, murr talking in the living room. Does Apa think I can be an important Park like our past grandfathers?

When Uhmma and Apa's bedroom door closes, I jump out of bed and run to the kitchen. I open the stuck drawer. It screams skeeee! It is hurt. My heart booms louder than the drums on the radio, but Uhmma and Apa do not open their bedroom door. I carefully pick out the flashlight Uncle Tim gave Apa for our first Mi Gook Christmas and slide in the drawer slow slow so it will not scream.

I run back to my room. Before I get back into bed, I say a quick prayer like I promised,

Thank you, God, for not telling Uhmma about the lie. Then all night, until my eyes do not want to stay open, I study for the Friday spelling test.

Being Older

Joon holds the yellow balloon with both hands like it is made of glass. It is his prize for being young.

Uhmma tells me, You are too old. Besides, why do you need a balloon? You already won an elephant.

I stare at my fuzzy pink, purple-nosed elephant and give the round body a little squeeze. It feels hard and crunchy as a bag of cereal.

I try to explain to Uhmma, This elephant is not what I want. I won it by mistake.

Uhmma stares off into the sparkly lights of the Ferris wheel and does not hear me. She pats the side of her face. I look at the ground, rub a piece of popcorn into the dirt. I want to tell her, I only took the prize because the man gave it to me, but I do not. I know Uhmma is still thinking about how Apa yelled and said there was no money for such foolishness like the fair. But Uhmma took us anyway. Because it was at my school, and everyone in my third-grade class would be there. Everyone except me.

A mistake. I did not mean to win when I threw the penny into the air. This elephant is worth only a penny. Not a whole fifty cents like Joon's yellow balloon. Besides, a stupid elephant can only sit and stare. A balloon can fly like birds touching the sky. Someday, I will find a tree that stretches to heaven. And when I climb it, all the fuzzy white lamb clouds will jump into my arms. They will whisper in my ear and tell me where to find Harabugi.

Uhmma's hand rests heavy on my head. She strokes my hair and says without looking away from her far-off place, Young Ju, you are the Uhn-nee. Be reasonable.

Her words make me small. Small in my heart because I do not want to be reasonable. I want Uhmma to buy me a balloon even though we have already spent too much money at a place we should not have been. I want to shout and cry, be the baby, not the Uhn-nee. But instead I nod.

Let us go, Uhmma says. I turn around one last time to look at all the things we could not do because we had only one line of tickets. Not a whole roll like John Chuchurelli's father, who sits on the bench in his blue suit, handing out tickets like tissues every time John and his sister run by.

People on the tilt-a-whirl scream long and loud, but then laugh that they are just playing.

z

w

u

A scary voice howls from the house with the crooked door and broken windows. The Ferris wheel chimes happy as an ice cream truck. The smell of pink sweet cloud candy makes my tongue wiggle in my mouth. Someday I will go on all the rides and eat anything I want. Even have lemonade instead of just water from the fountain.

I get in the front of the car with Uhmma. Joon sits in the back. Joon keeps the balloon on his lap, holding it with both hands. Uhmma drives away from the fair without a prize, only a deep fingerprint between her eyebrows. I want to touch it and see if it will go away, but Uhmma will just tell me to sit still. I turn backward in my seat and lean over to bother Joon.

Why do you not let the balloon go and hold it by the string? I ask.

Uhmma told me if I am not careful it will fly away, Joon says.

It is on a string and we are in the car, dong boy. It is not going far.

Joon hugs the balloon tighter.

Here, let me hold the string, I say.

No, he says, his eyes dark and tight.

Balloons are supposed to fly. They like to be free, I tell him. What good is a balloon if you never let it go?

My balloon. Not yours, Uhn-nee, Joon

says, trying to wiggle away from my hand.

Come on. You have to share.

No.

I will trade you my elephant, I say, swinging the fat pink, purple-nosed cereal ball by its ear.

Joon does not look up, just holds the balloon.

Please, Joon, I say. I will not let it go. Please. I just want to see it fly a little.

No. It is my balloon. Joon gives me a mean look that turns him into Apa.

I hope it flies away, I say and lean way over to pinch him on the arm.

Uhmma! Joon cries.

Uhmma jumps a little like she is waking up from a dream. Young Ju, what are you doing? Uhmma scolds. Turn around and leave your brother alone.

Yes, Uhmma, I say and turn back around in my seat. I hold the elephant in my lap, crunch his body. Maybe he will get softer if I play with him. I stare out the window for the rest of the ride and call out the road signs I can read.

"Next exit!" I yell. "Santa Monica Freeway!"

When Uhmma turns off the freeway, I see our house that is not really our house. Apa still says that someday we will buy a house of our own. For now we are renting. For now has been a long time.

As soon as Uhmma stops the car, I grab my elephant and jump out. I run for the house, swinging my elephant around and around my head. Behind me, I hear the car door slam. Just as I reach the front door there is a sound. *Pung!* Loud as the time Uncle Tim opened up the big bottle and white sea foam came spilling out.

I turn around.

Joon lies face down on the driveway. The balloon is gone. Joon pushes himself off the ground. He stands up holding a string with broken egg yolk on the end.

Balloon! Joon cries.

Uhmma bends down, rubs his back. She says, Joon Ho, stop crying. I will get you a new balloon another time.

My balloon, Joon cries. I want my balloon!

Shhh, Joon Ho. Stop now. Let us go inside. Uhmma grabs his hand and tries to lead him away. Joon puts both his hands on Uhmma's leg and pushes her back. He opens his mouth even bigger.

I want my *balloon!*

Snot runs down from his nose into his mouth. Uhmma closes her eyes. She closes her eyes and does not open them. One hand reaches up and covers half her face. The other hand knots together. Two knuckles sticking out.

Thump.

Balloon! Joon cries louder *Balloon! Balloon!*

Uhmma's eyes search the sky. She raises her knuckles to thump him again but then changes her mind. She hides behind her hands. Like she can disappear.

I hear a knocking. I look up. Mr. Owner is staring out the upstairs window, pointing at Joon. Knock. Point, point. I am scared. Why does Uhmma let Joon stand there? What is wrong with her?

I look at my fat pink, purple-nosed elephant. Even though he is not a balloon, he is the only thing I have from the fair. My prize for being older.

I walk over to Joon. Use my best English teacher voice. The way Mrs. Russo talks to crybaby kids who fall down on the playground. "Joon, please do not cry. You are a big boy now."

Joon stops crying and watches my mouth make the strange words.

"You will be fine," I say.

Joon does not understand my words. His mouth opens up to cry again.

Here, Joon, I say and quickly put the elephant in his hands. This will not break, I say. See? I poke the elephant in his fat stomach.

Joon closes his mouth and stares at the elephant.

See, you can play with him, I say, crunching his body. Come on. Let us go make him a fort.

My elephant, Joon says. He kisses the purple nose.

No, Joon. It is still mine. You can play with him.

Mine, Joon says and starts walking to the front door.

Uhmma puts down her hands and opens her eyes. She watches me. I keep my eyes on her as I follow Joon back to the house.

Disappearing Bubbles

Sometimes Amanda says things I do not understand. Yesterday she told me that she and her parents went apple picking and they had doughnuts and hot cider. "I love cider," Amanda said. "Don't you?"

I nodded and said yes, even though I did not know what cider was. Amanda has been my best friend ever since the time I lied about Joon dying and she gave me a Lifesaver, but that does not mean I tell her everything.

I lie in bed, stare up at the ceiling, and think about the dictionary definition of cider — juice pressed from apples. How is cider different from apple juice? What is fermenting? I have found that the dictionary doesn't always explain everything. Like "going." Ever since the beginning of fourth grade, Amanda and some of the girls in my class talk about going with this boy, Jimmy. "Who do you think he wants to go with?" they ask. I pretend to understand, but in the dictionary it says "go" and "going" mean action, moving, and lots of other things like business transactions. None of it makes any sense to me. Where would

Jimmy go with someone?

There is a quick knock on the door and then Apa pokes in his head. Young Ju, Apa says, time to get out of bed now. We must wash the car.

Yes, Apa, I answer and slowly get up.

Outside, on the driveway, Apa has already set out the white bucket and sponges next to the car. The houses around us are all quiet and dark, everyone still sleeping at seven o'clock on a Sunday morning. Joon walks out from the house and comes over to me. After a second of standing quietly, he reaches down and picks up the dishwashing soap. He squeezes it onto his hands.

"Joon. Stop that," I say and grab the yellow bottle away from him. "That's for the car."

Young Ju, Apa orders as he drags a green hose from the side of the house, speak Korean.

I do not understand why I have to speak Korean at home so I will not forget where I come from. Why did we move to America if I am to speak English only at school? But I do not argue with Apa. Instead I tell Joon, Stand here. I move him off to the side and give him a sponge to hold.

Apa calls out, Young Ju, go turn on the water.

I run around to the side of the house and

turn on the faucet full blast. When I get back to the driveway, Apa is filling up the bucket with water. Joon stands next to him holding the yellow bottle, squeezing too much dishwashing soap into the bucket. Joon looks up as I walk toward them. He sticks out his tongue at me.

Remember, Apa reminds me as he sprays the station wagon with water, scrub fast so the bubbles will not dry before we rinse.

Apa says this every time we wash the car. Something about the paint peeling if we do not do it just right. Even though Uncle Tim gave us the station wagon a long time ago and it is so old the fake wood side panels are peeling off, Apa treats it like we bought it yesterday.

Get ready, he yells over his shoulder.

Joon, hold this, I order and give him a pink sponge. I show him how to get ready — knees bent, sponge in hand, waiting for Apa's signal.

As soon as Apa drops the hose, he yells, *Go!* I smack the side of the car with my sponge. Soap bubbles run down the peeling panels.

Apa calls from the other side of the car, Get the tire, Young Ju.

I kneel down and scrub a hubcap.

When I finish with it, I stand up to find Joon picking up the bubbles that have floated down the driveway and collected in the gutter. He piles the bubbles together like he is making a sand castle.

Joon, come back here and help, I call out.

Joon ignores me and keeps playing with the bubbles.

I start to walk down the driveway. Joon, I call. Come here. Now!

Yah, Young Ju, Apa says to me over the roof of the car. Leave him alone. He is doing his own work. Come soap the car before the bubbles dry.

Playing with bubbles is work? When I was Joon's age, I had to help Uhmma and Apa as much as I could. I had regular chores like folding laundry and setting the table.

I walk back to the car and begin to soap the hood. My arms stretch out as far as possible and still they reach only halfway across the hood. Already the bubbles are starting to dry.

Hurry up, Apa orders. He bulldozes past me and covers the rest of the hood with suds. I sigh and start working on the bumper.

I hate being the smallest in my class. Being the first person in the front row for pictures. Unless they know me, kids think I'm in the second grade. All of us in my family look like tangerines next to oranges. All of us except Joon. Joon is tall for his age. Uhmma and Apa admire his huge feet and say, You are going to be the tall one in the family. I wish I could be the tall one. Tall as Amanda and not worry about what cider tastes like or what going means.

I have to pee, Joon shouts from the curb.

Go inside, Apa tells him without missing a swipe with his soapy sponge.

I do not want to, Joon calls back. I am peeing right here.

I look up and see Joon pulling down his shorts. Apa is washing the rear bumper and does not see him.

Apa. Joon is going to the bathroom outside, I say.

Apa does not even look up.

With his shorts bunched at his knees, Joon holds his go-chu with both hands. A tip of his tongue hangs out, covering his bottom lip. He is concentrating.

A Big Wheel grinds down the street.

Someone is coming, Joon, I yell, hoping to stop him before it is too late.

Joon looks up, sticks his tongue out even farther, and shoots a clear line of pee into his pile of bubbles. A boy with peach-fuzz blond hair and denim overalls gets off his Big Wheel to watch. I hurry over to tell Apa about how Joon is embarrassing the family. The whole neighborhood will think we are stranger than we already look. For once, I am glad my school is so far from home. At least no one I know will have seen Joon.

Apa, I say, Joon cannot go to the bathroom in the middle of the street.

Apa stops soaping the car and turns around to look at Joon.

Apa, you have to stop him, I say.

Young Ju, Apa says, shaking his head. Joon Ho is a boy. It is natural for him to pee outside.

I don't understand why Apa thinks boys and girls cannot be treated the same. Why they are so different. There is no dictionary for these kinds of questions.

Joon, now that he has an audience, starts to do tricks. He waves his go-chu back and forth like a fireman hosing down a burning house. Peach Fuzz just stares.

Apa starts to laugh. Joon Ho, who do you think you are? A fireman?

Yes, I am, Joon says. He shakes his go-chu clear of the last drops and pulls up his shorts. Peach Fuzz scratches his head and leans forward to see if the mound of bubbles has disappeared. Joon stands with his hands on his hips like he is challenging the kid to do better.

Joon orders Peach Fuzz around in Korean. Peach Fuzz nods as though he understands and the two of them build a mound of bubbles. Apa kneels and soaps the last two tires on the station wagon. I stand by the car, the soapy sponge still in my hand, and gaze off at the street, empty and long, stretching far into the distance.

For one second, the time it takes to blink, I imagine throwing my sponge into the air. Running fast, fast down the street. So fast that I begin to fly. Away. From here. From me.

But when I open my eyes, I am still standing in my place next to Apa. I turn my head so I do not have to watch him spray down the car and make the bubbles disappear.

The Blob

On some weekend mornings, not always, hardly even any, but some, Apa becomes the Blob. He wakes up with broom hair and catches Joon and me watching cartoons. He sneaks up from behind and scoops us up all at once like a fisherman with a net. We scream and laugh, try to break free, but his lock-strong arms keep us in jail.

Uhmma! we screech. Uhmma, help! We are trapped.

Uhmma comes out of the kitchen, smiles, but shows us her hands. I cannot help you, she says. I will get caught too.

Nooo! the Blob yells and catches a wiggling Joon by the ankle just as he is about to escape. He stuffs Joon under his arm as easy as a squirrel hiding an acorn. Joon and I try to join forces, like Spider-Man and Superman, like Wonder Twin Powers Activate! Form of a tickle torture. Get him!

Oh no, the Blob does not have a ticklish spot, not even under the arms. But we do. Under our arms. Below our chins. Around our bellies. Help, help! we laugh and gasp.

75

You can never get away, the Blob cackles and then farts, not once but three times, loud as a rusty car starting in the morning. Brumm. Brumm. Brumm.

Ahhh, we scream and try to plug our noses.

Never, the Blob yells and pins our arms so that we cannot raise our hands to our faces.

Uhmma! we yell again. Uhmma comes out of the kitchen once more. She sees we are almost out of breath. She cautiously approaches the Blob that stinks of last night's kimchi stew. She pokes his back with her finger.

Rooourrr! the Blob growls and reaches out to grab Uhmma's ankles. She jumps out of the way and runs for the kitchen. Returning with a towel coiled and ready for combat, she swipes the Blob's butt. He farts again just to make a point.

We are dying! I moan.

Hurry, Joon says, his face red and twisted with effort.

Uhmma grabs the Blob's shoulders and pulls him back like a weed. Joon and I try to crawl free, but the Blob catches our legs and pulls us back. He snatches the towel from Uhmma and pulls her into his kingdom by the hem of her shirt. There is no chance of escape. Now we are all one big Blob.

76

Do you give up? the Blob asks. Do you? Say it.

Never, we cry.

Take this, the Blob says and squeezes us tight as saved money.

Deh suh. We give up, we say.

Good.

When it feels like no air can ever pass through our mouths even though they are wide open from laughing, the Blob finally lets us go. His body goes limp and he melts into the carpet. We lift off his heavy limbs, crawl free.

Ohh, ha, ha, hee. Whee, Apa laughs and gasps at the same time. He gets up slowly. Pats Joon and me on the head. Even pats Uhmma on the shoulder. As he shuffles off to the bathroom, Apa picks up the Korean newspaper from the coffee table and tucks it under his arm.

Sometimes after Apa leaves we have a carpet burn on our knee. Or a bruise on our arm. But that does not matter. We still wait and wait. Hope and hope. Like watching the sky for snow on Christmas even though the sun shines hot all year round. Because when the Blob comes and wraps us tight in his arms, holds us so close we can hardly breathe, that is when we can finally put our arms around him.

Rainy-Day Surprises

Rain splatters over the car. Joon and I are jailed inside with only a soccer ball and one old library book. Joon lies flat on his stomach, taking up the whole back seat. He hangs his chin over the edge of the seat and picks lint off the car floor. He piles the lint on top of the hump that makes the border for feet space.

Usually it is not this bad on Thursdays and Fridays, when Uhmma and Apa both work late at their second jobs. Waiting for Uhmma at Johnny's Steak House is better than "Please do not touch that" if we wait at Gomo's house. Next year, when I am old enough, Uhmma says I can watch Joon all by myself at home.

When it is not raining, Joon and I play in the alley behind the restaurant, next to the open door of the kitchen. We can bounce the soccer ball against the gray walls until the manager comes outside and says, "Cut out that racket." Then we play two-square and make up our own rules like No Bounce, Around the Back, and Sky Ball.

And right before the sun goes down, before the rush of knives chopping, food flying, and "Order ready!" singing out, Uhmma will come out of the kitchen and give us our dinner. If we are lucky, it might be ginger chicken, spicy hot, fire on the tongue. But most times it is soup and rice in a bowl, all mixed together so you can eat it with one big spoon. Joon and I sit on the curb with our bowls balanced on our knees, slurping like we are not supposed to at the dinner table. We laugh and see who can make the grossest noise.

But today, because it is raining and the cars are pulling off the freeway quick quick for a long, early dinner, Uhmma can only rush out with two dry old hamburgers and a big carton of milk. After we finish our dinner, Joon can't sit still. He crawls around in the back seat sticking his hand down between the seat cushions for change. After he finds only two dimes, Joon bounces the soccer ball off the ceiling and starts to sing. Soon the whole car is rocking with his crazy song. "Spider-Man. Spider-Man. He can do what no one can."

I turn on the flashlight and read him a story about Frog and Toad to make him be good. He bounces the ball against his knee and laughs at all the funny parts. When the book ends we shine the light out the window. We watch the rain hit the black tar and bounce back up like a million tiny silver grasshoppers.

After a while Joon yawns and lets the ball fall to the floor. He curls up in the back seat, one arm under his head. A calm, slow breathing fills the air. I turn off the flashlight and sit in Uhmma's seat. Even though it is raining, the kitchen door is wide open. Inside, people rush back and forth carrying plates. I keep my eyes on the door and think about the last rainy day.

That time the storm was so strong, Uhmma had to hold the umbrella with two hands. She came to the car and tapped softly on the window and I was the only one awake. I opened the door. Uhmma asked, Are you still hungry?

Yes, I whispered even though my stomach felt full. She put her arm around my shoulders and led me out of the car. She closed the door quietly so as not to wake Joon and locked up the car.

Uhmma whispered, The manager went up front for a break. You can come inside for a little while.

When I stepped into the kitchen, steamy fingers of steak and garlic drew me farther inside. Faces from the stove and sink turned to smile, but then moved so fast their words trailed like smoke from a train.

"Suna-san, you girl amai," said the woman

80

who flipped the steaks on the grill.

"Pretty girl you got, Suna," sang a waitress with curly sunray hair. She picked up her orders, placing them three plates across on one arm, and headed for the door.

"How old you?" asked the old cook with crescent-shaped eyes and night spreading his two front teeth. Uhmma had told me about this Chinese cook before. He knew how to take away a headache just by pushing a certain place on your palm. "Ten," I said. And then because he giggled, I held up both hands and showed him all of my fingers. He gave my fingers a tug.

"You wanee somu soupu?" he asked, pretending to slurp from a bowl. I nodded my happiness and waited for my reward of a small, warm bowl.

I carried my bowl to a table tucked in the back of the kitchen. Uhmma sat drinking tea with the woman who worked at the grill. Grill Woman's hair was wrapped tight on top of her head, pulling her eyes up at the corners. Uhmma patted the seat next to her and continued talking to her friend. I sat down and sipped quietly at my soup.

Uhmma and Grill Woman spoke in a language of mixed and chopped Korean and Japanese, glued together with pieces of English.

"Suna, kinoo that ahjimma scratch car,"

81

Grill Woman said, her eyes small and bright, the size of new pennies.

"Aigoo. Fix takai?"

"No, scratch chiisai." Grill Woman picked up her cup of tea with her pinkie sticking straight out. I watched her pinkie dance in the air. Uhmma held her cup with both hands, blowing into the steam before each sip. I looked at my hands holding the bowl of soup. Just like Uhmma's. I blew into my bowl and took a sip.

Uhmma was quick to laugh at all of her friend's words. Her squeaky-shoes laugh was back and her face shone bright as a full moon on cold, clear nights. Sometimes when she was speaking fast, she put her cup down and her hands waved and danced in the steamy air. This was a different Uhmma. Not a sad, tired Uhmma who cooked and cleaned and sometimes yelled, but a stranger who had a friend and a secret language all her own. Not my Uhmma. A Suna.

All around me the pots clanked, knives stomped, and the sound of sizzling steak swirled through the air. The waitress with the sunray hair came back through the swinging doors. She held out two bubbly pink drinks, each with a cherry, red as candy, floating in the ice.

"Here, Suna, I brought you and your

daughter your favorite drink. A Shirley Temple." The waitress winked at Uhmma as she set down the drinks.

"Oh, tank you, Kim-bru-rie," Uhmma said. Uhmma pushed one drink toward me and picked up the other, raising it high in the air. She waited for me to copy.

We clinked glasses just like people in the movies. Uhmma took a sip of the magic drink, then smacked her lips. I took a sip and felt the familiar sting of fizz but with the sweetness of cherries and sunshine all mixed together. I smacked my lips and looked up at Uhmma.

Good? she asked.

Good, I said.

Outside the rain kept falling. A few of the waitresses complained it was miserable weather. Everyone in the kitchen agreed. I bowed my head, watched the cherry float around in my glass. If I could have had one wish, right then, a genie ready for an order, I would have asked that the rain fall forever.

Now Joon wakes up and kicks the back of the driver's seat. "I hate rainy days. Where is Uhmma? I want to go home." Joon kicks the seat a few more times and then becomes quiet again.

I watch the open kitchen door and do not say anything. I like rainy days.

Strong Is a Man

Joon and Spencer sit sweating under the sun in the middle of the outside cement patio. Pieces of a Lego village are scattered all around them. They are so busy clicking the small gray blocks together that they do not hear me slide open the backyard glass door. They have one tower built, and Spencer checks the box to make sure they are building the second tower just like in the medieval castle in the picture.

"Joon," I call from the doorway, "we have to go to Gomo's house now."

Joon looks up at the sound of my voice, but then with a scowl focuses back on the blocks in his hands.

I hear Apa calling to me from the living room, Is Joon Ho ready to go?

"Joon," I say again, "it's time to go."

Joon stays kneeling on the cement floor. Apa comes from behind me to the sliding glass doorway.

Joon, clean up, Apa says.

Joon pretends he does not hear and busily snaps a block into place. Apa grabs the edge of the open door frame, the smell of bleach and Windex from cleaning the lawyers' offices last night still lingering on his hands. He pushes me aside and walks over to Joon.

Joon still does not look up from the Legos but begins to complain, I hate going to Gomo's house for lunch. Why do we have to go? It is so boring. All we do is sit. There is nothing for us to play with there. I have no fun.

I stand in the doorway, unable to leave even though I know what is going to happen next.

Joon Ho, get up, Apa orders, standing over him.

Joon tilts his head back and then scrambles up on his feet.

You are whining like a girl, Apa says and cuffs Joon on the head.

Joon's eyes squint against the pain, but more than that, the humiliation of being punished in public, in front of his friend.

Spencer turns away, rubs the side of his crewcut white-blond hair with the back of his knuckles. He has had the same haircut for as long as he and Joon have been friends.

Apa notices Spencer's movements and gives him a wide, only-for-guests smile. "Shupen-cher," Apa says. "Time you go home now. Joon Ho back soon."

"Sure, Mr. Park," Spencer says, ducking

his head and rubbing the fuzz above his ear.

"Good boy," Apa says, the same smile stuck to his face.

"See ya, Joon." Spencer takes off around the side of the house, leaving behind his Lego set.

Apa waits for Spencer to disappear and then turns back to Joon. The smile flies off his lips faster than a door slamming.

Joon keeps his head bowed, his hands clenching and unclenching by his side.

Apa steps closer to Joon. Yah, look at me when I am talking to you.

Joon lifts his face. His eyes glower.

Wipe that look off your face, Apa orders.

Joon's face twitches as he tries to recompose himself, tries to relax the corners of his eyes and focus on something over Apa's shoulder. I know the technique, how to look blank and as if you are listening when really you are trying to fly away from your body. You can't let Apa know what you are thinking or it will be worse.

What have I told you about whining?

Do not whine, Joon repeats from a well-heard speech.

What else? Apa asks, stepping even closer.

Only girls whine. Men are stronger than that.

Good. Then why were you acting like a girl?

I do not know, Joon says, his eyes holding a corner of the sky.

You mean you forgot, Apa says and pokes Joon in the chest with the tip of his finger.

Joon stumbles back for a second and then rights himself.

You forgot, Apa says again, stepping in closer, making up for the lost ground.

Joon nods, his eyes tearing over even though he is holding on to that corner of sky like it is a line to heaven.

Say the truth, Apa orders.

I forgot, Joon drones.

Say it all, Apa snarls, biting down on his lower lip.

I forgot how to be a man, Joon says. A betraying tear slides down his face and Joon hurries to brush it off.

What are you crying for?

Joon shrugs.

Wrong answer. Apa slams his hand across Joon's face.

Joon's head jolts back. A howl escapes from his lips.

Uhmma comes to the doorway and stands behind me. She calls out to Apa over my head, Yuhboh, that is enough.

Apa turns toward her voice. Shut up, Apa says. Keep out of it. This is my son and he will not grow up weak.

Yuhboh, Uhmma says again.

Apa ignores her and focuses back on Joon. Stand up straight, Apa orders.

Joon straightens up, wiping the tears from his face, looking around for that corner of sky.

You cry like a girl. You whine like a girl. Have I not taught you anything? Be strong. Be a man.

Joon's face grows blank again. He found it.

Apa continues, In this world, only the strong survive. Only the strong can make their future. If you cry and whine like a girl, who is going to listen to you? Who? If you talk like a man, fight like a man, you will get what you want in this world. Do you understand?

Yes, Joon whispers.

What did you say? Apa leans in, ear offered up as though listening for a mouse in the wall.

Yes, Joon says louder.

Yes, and what else? Apa asks, straightening up.

It is important for Joon to get it right. If he says what Apa wants to hear, the lecture will end. If he gets it wrong?

Joon hardens the muscles of his face. A mask of glass covers his eyes, cheeks, lips, forehead. Joon says clearly, I must talk like a man and fight like a man if I want to make my future.

Apa leans back on his heels, clasps his

88

hands behind him. Good, Apa says. Good.

My held-in breath pops out from my chest in relief.

Joon looks in my direction.

Apa turns as if to leave and then pivots back around. He balances on one leg and swiftly kicks Joon in the stomach.

Joon never saw it. Never got to prepare his body. The mask of glass explodes into fine shards of pain, etching his face unrecognizable, old. In Joon's place stands a prune-faced grandfather, stooped, holding his stomach, unable to walk.

Uhmma pushes me to the side and rushes out to Joon. Apa grabs her by the shoulder and stops her in one abrupt movement. Joon's mouth gapes wide open as he fights for air.

Apa shoves Uhmma in front of him as they turn back to the house. Apa says calmly, He has to learn his lesson.

Apa stops at the scattered Lego set and tells Joon, Hurry and clean that up before we leave for your Gomo's. I do not want to be late.

Joon hobbles over to the Legos.

I back away as Apa and Uhmma step inside. After they pass, I rush outside and help Joon clean up. We kneel together and disassemble the castle towers.

"I hate him," Joon says.

I nod silently and drop the small gray plastic pieces back into the box. As I try to pull apart a red flag from a gray block, the flag breaks in my hand.

Joon's eyes follow the sound of the snap. "That's my flag!" Joon cries and jerks back his hand.

I stare at the broken flag in my palm. Joon's slap rings in my ear.

Harry

We thought nothing would happen the way we wanted. Not ever.

Not the time Apa, with a distant edge in his eye, took us to see the new houses being built on a nearby hill and said, We shall see. But then we never did see, although Joon and I asked every day and even packed our clothes in brown paper grocery bags in case we had to move fast.

Not the time a letter addressed to Apa with the words "You Are the Next Ten-Million-Dollar Winner!" and two hazy men's grins stamped on the front made Joon and me so crazy with heat we had to run up and down the hallway screaming.

And definitely not the time Harry died. It's hardest to think of Harry because we tried that time. Really tried. It wasn't about luck or waiting for Uhmma and Apa to tell us the good news. It was about us. Joon and me trying our best, like the teachers in school tell us to do and we'll be rewarded. Even then. Nothing.

Harry was our baby bird, an orphan we had

to save because we found him crying all alone with no one to take care of him. He was worse off than we were. Joon found him on the way home from the corner market one day. As always, Joon was running ahead of me, gathering up speed on the downhill so that he could jump over a low juniper bush. Joon leapt forward, and then just as it looked like he might clear, his back foot caught a branch.

I think it was fate that made Joon fall when he tried to jump over that bush. If Joon's head hadn't been so close to the ground the moment Harry peeped for help, we would never have found him. He was such a little bird. Nothing but a spit mark on the dirt.

When we got Harry home, Joon and I made up some juk-rice and warm water all mixed together looking like glue. It was the food Uhmma fed us when we were sick. Every time Harry opened his mouth we fed him a spoonful of juk. After a while Harry was covered with it, but he stopped crying and fell asleep.

Joon didn't think Uhmma and Apa should know about Harry. "He's our bird, Uhn-nee. We have to take care of him." Joon's eyebrows knitted together in a dark scowl. "Anyway, they might not let us keep him."

So we wrapped Harry in an old towel and put him in a shoe-box. We hid him in the back of Joon's closet. Ellie, the purple-nosed elephant, stood guard. We tried to love Harry the way good parents are supposed to. We cooed and petted his short, dark feathers. We held him next to our cheeks and told him he was going to grow up to be a strong bird.

After school, we would "guy-bye-boh" to see who had to clean out the box and who got to feed Harry.

"Ready?" I asked Joon.

"Ready."

"Guy. Bye. Boh." We shook our fists in rhythm to the words.

Joon held out his hand flat. Paper.

I held out two fingers in a V. Scissors. Scissors cut paper.

"I win," I said and gently scooped up Harry. Joon picked up the box, his head angled away from the odor.

"When do you think we should teach him to fly?" I asked as I spooned some juk into Harry's mouth.

"Soon, I think," Joon said, scraping out the inside of the box with a crumpled piece of paper. He turned to me with a grin. "I bet Harry's going to grow to be an eagle."

I looked at Harry's skinny neck. I didn't know about that, but I didn't say anything.

When Harry got to be a little bigger, Joon cupped him in his hands and zoomed around the house.

"I'm teaching him how it feels to have the wind in his face," Joon said when I worried Harry might get dizzy. I sat on the couch hugging my knees, fingers crossed in hope that Joon would not crash into a wall. I knew Harry had to learn how to be a bird someday. He was growing fast.

But then he stopped. Growing. Breathing. We opened the closet door and Harry didn't peep when the light reached him. I took out the box. Harry lay curled up in the towel, still and quiet as the sunlight falling on the bed. I didn't want to believe what I saw. I closed my eyes. Maybe Harry would move when I opened my eyes again. No. I started to cry and looked over at Joon. He stood stiff and straight, staring at the wall above his bed, clenching and unclenching his fists. I touched his shoulder. Joon jerked away.

We buried Harry on a hill, the hill where we were supposed to live but never got a chance to. We wanted Harry to be someplace high so he could at least have a clear view of the sky. And even though there were brand-new houses all around the place we were headed, we tried to walk as if we belonged there in our patched jeans and tight, faded T-shirts, carrying an old shoebox and a purple-nosed elephant. No one stopped us.

We knew there were no houses in one area

of the hill, only a few trees and crumbling dirt. With the sun dying at our backs, Joon and I knelt down with our spoons and started to dig. A light breeze stirred the ground and a mist of dirt rose up, coating our faces, hair, and the inside of our noses.

As the sun dipped below the horizon and night waited high in the sky, I placed Harry's box into the hole. Joon settled Ellie on top to stand guard. When the last of Ellie's pink fur disappeared underground, Joon and I stood up and put the spoons back in our pockets. Black lines of dirt rimmed the tips of my nails. I tried picking some of it out but only pushed it farther in. Frustrated, I shoved my hands quickly into my pockets. I glanced over at Joon.

Joon's head was tilted down, and there was barely a rise in his chest when he breathed. His eyes were locked on the small mound no bigger than a teddy-bear bump under the covers. Maybe it was the faint light or the way Joon, who was never still, did not even move his hands, but for a moment I thought I was seeing his ghost. I tried to bring him back.

"Let's pray like they do on TV and in church," I said, remembering the way Halmoni's prayers and rocking always made me feel better.

"Why?" Joon said, lifting his chin.

"Well, when people die, they say prayers to thank God and —"

"God hasn't done anything that I should have to thank him for."

I didn't know how to respond to that, so I went around it. "Maybe we could just say something about Harry. It doesn't have to be a prayer."

Joon shrugged but stayed where he was. I licked my lips and started. "Harry, we're really sorry you had to go away. We were going to teach you how to fly and everything. I'm sorry if we didn't give you enough food or take care of you like a real mommy bird would have." I could feel the tears coming, so I sputtered out quickly, "Good-bye, Harry."

Joon rubbed his hands along the sides of his jeans. He kept rubbing them as if they were never going to get clean. I cried quietly, but Joon never uttered a sound. As my tears dried and the silence spread between us until I thought there was nothing more to say, I turned to leave.

In a broken whisper, Joon finally spoke. "I love you, Harry," Joon said. His eyes searched the stars. "It never happens the way we want. Never."

One Hundred Pennies

Please, Uhmma. It only takes a dollar, I explain.

Uhmma stares at the orange and white form filled with numbers.

The twenty-three-million-dollar sign makes me brave with my words. I tell her, We could win and then we would be rich.

I see Uhmma figuring out the cost in her head. She rubs the sheet between her fingers as if it were an expensive piece of silk.

Uhmma says that in America even one penny should be saved. When Uhmma caught me throwing a penny, along with old papers, in the trash, she yelled, Do you think the clerk would let me leave with the groceries when I am one penny short?

I argued back, even though I wasn't supposed to. Uhmma, it is only a penny. You cannot buy anything for a penny.

Uhmma narrowed her eyes. You were born to the wrong family. You should be with parents who can afford to throw away pennies like trash.

Uhmma loves her pennies, collects them

like flowers in an old glass vase she found at a garage sale. More than once Uhmma's pennies have saved the weekly groceries. I am embarrassed when Uhmma puts down a million pennies and the clerk snarls as she counts out the change. I inch away from Uhmma, pretend I am not that woman's daughter. Not a poor Oriental who saves pennies like gold.

Uhmma starts digging at the bottom of her purse for the change that will buy us a ticket to our dreams. Go ahead, she says. Get us a ticket.

"Yes!" I shout, and hurry to fill in the numbers.

I color in the bubble next to my favorite number, 11, for the day I was born. I tap the pen against my lips and think about other lucky numbers. I remember the seven days Harry lived and fill in the bubble next to the number 7. I know he will help us win. Just to be nice, I pick the number 17, for the day Joon was born. Three more numbers.

Uhmma, do you have a favorite number? I ask.

Uhmma looks up and purses her lips for a second, and then a slow smile spreads across her face, erasing the faint, squinting worry lines between her eyes. She says quietly, Ten. I like the number ten.

I start to ask her why that number, but

Uhmma has already gone back to scraping up the change in her purse. I carefully fill in the oval next to the number 10 for Uhmma. What number would Apa like? Apa with his yellow callused palms from gardening all day and then cleaning up the lawyers' offices at night. The pen hovers over the numbers, unsure of where to go. Finally, I dot in the oval next to the number 1. One for being the only Apa I have. One for being the only son who must send money back to Halmoni.

And finally 23, for all the millions that will make us magically better. No more closed-door, late-night arguing over money. No more bowls loaded with fluffy white rice hiding small pieces of meat. No more saving pennies. I finish filling out the sheet and wave it at Uhmma, who stands there cupping in two hands a chance at our dreams.

At the counter I lay down the Superlotto sheet and look over the six glowing blue dots.

"One Superlotto ticket, please," I say.

Uhmma puts down her change: one quarter, two dimes, five nickels, and too many pennies. I wrinkle my nose at all the pennies and try to look elsewhere as the woman behind the counter watches Uhmma count. I try to fill my head with all the things that will happen when we are rich.

On the drive home, nothing is impossible. I

ask Uhmma, What would you do if we won the lottery?

Oh, I suppose I would buy everyone some new shoes, she says and looks down at my sneakers that pinch at the toes.

Sneakers! I cry. Sneakers are nothing with twenty-three million dollars. You could buy a new car or even a house with all that money! I think about the houses on the hill, the ones with lollipop-green grass and not one but *two* front doors with gold handles.

Yes, Uhmma says, but how comfortable would you be if your feet hurt?

I hate when Uhmma makes too much sense. I try to get her to think big. What kind of car would you get, Uhmma?

She thinks about it for a while, peering carefully at the cars rushing by. An Oldsmobile, she says.

An Oldsmobile? You mean those big grandfather cars that take up two lanes?

Yes.

Those cars are too big, Uhmma. What about a Mercedes or a Porsche? I ask, imagining Uhmma and me in a fast, sleek Porsche.

Uhmma shakes her head and then checks her blind spot before changing lanes.

An Oldsmobile, Uhmma explains, is safe and roomy. It is big enough to hold a whole family. You know my friend Kay, at the restaurant, she says that she saw an accident between an Oldsmobile and a Toyota. The Toyota was bent and completely broken, but the Oldsmobile had only a scratch on its bumper. Uhmma's eyes grow wide. She takes one hand off the steering wheel and points to a black Oldsmobile speeding in the carpool lane. Uhmma turns to me. That is the kind of car I would like to drive someday, she says.

I think about the Oldsmobile, strong enough to bulldoze regular cars, probably even station wagons. Certainly a station wagon whose right back door flies open when you take left turns too quick, gets honked at every time it inches up a hill, and leaks black oil all over the street. A beat-up station wagon is no match for an Oldsmobile.

While Uhmma drives, I sit dreaming of closets filled with brand-new clothes still smelling of department store perfume, cupboards filled with Entenmann's cakes, and boxes and boxes of real cereal, not the fake kind with yellow writing. I dream of an Oldsmobile and a Porsche sitting in a spacious garage lined with shelves and neatly hung tools.

When we get home, I run to my room to look at my social studies book with its pictures of the world. My fingers trace the maps while I read the names of faraway places: New Zealand, Greece, France, Italy, Japan, Korea. I lie on my bed imagining an ocean breeze on my face as I travel the world on a ship. I would swim in those jellybean-shaped pools and sip lemonade under the hot sun.

"Young Ju, dinner time," Joon yells, poking his head into my room. He burps and then slams the door. My ship is back home.

All through dinner I twist in my seat, checking the clock to make sure I do not miss the hour of magic numbers. I know the channel and time by heart from watching the show every Saturday after the *Six O'Clock News Hour* with Michael Markson.

Apa growls under his breath, Young Ju, stop turning around. Eat your dinner politely.

I sit up straight and try to finish my dinner quickly. I clank my spoon against the bowl, scraping the sticky rice from the sides.

Young Ju! Apa says, pointing his chopsticks at me. How many times do I have to remind you that it is not polite to make noises when cleaning your bowl? Do it over again.

My shoulders slump. I try as carefully and as quietly as possible to scrape the rice kernels that cling like drowning victims to the sides of the bowl. We can never leave the table until every last one is eaten. When I finish, I glance at Uhmma. She checks my bowl and nods.

Back in my room, I stare at the old alarm clock that ticks too loud at night. Fifteen more minutes. I cross my fingers, wishing with all my might that Apa will soon get up from the table and go away so that I can turn on the TV in the living room. Soon I hear the front door slam. Apa has gone outside for his after-dinner cigarette. I bolt from my room.

"Hurry up, Joon! We are about to win twenty-three million dollars," I shout on my way to the living room.

"What are you talking about?" Joon asks, standing in the hallway.

"Look, look!" I take the orange and white ticket with the six magic numbers out of Uhmma's purse. I wave it at him as though I am cheering on my team at the Olympics.

"We're not going to win," Joon scoffs, but he plops down on the sofa anyway.

"Yes, we are! I feel it already," I say. And I do. I can feel the scream of happiness waiting in my belly.

Uhmma, I call as I flick on the TV, do you not want to watch?

You tell me when it comes on and I will come over, she yells over the noise of running water and clanking dishes.

I turn the knob to Channel 7 and there is Michael Markson in a tie with blue stripes. He jokes for a little bit and then signs off. After a few commercials, an announcer wearing a black and white suit with a bow tie at his neck comes on to say the winning numbers.

Uhmma, I call out, it is starting!

Uhmma rushes to the living room still rubbing her hands dry on a towel. She sits on the edge of the couch, leaning forward, her eyes blinking at the screen.

"Here are the winning numbers for this week's twenty-three-million-dollar jackpot," the announcer says swiftly. The numbered balls jump around in the cage, then one falls forward.

"Ten," his voice booms. I squeal my happy surprise and point to the lucky number on my sheet.

"Nineteen, thirty-one, twenty-seven, fourteen, thirty-nine. This week's lucky numbers are ten, fourteen, nineteen, twenty-seven, thirty-one, thirty-nine. Thank you for playing Superlotto."

The winning numbers hover in the middle of the screen, suspended against a brilliant blue background. I check the numbers against the sheet in my hand. I cannot point to any number except 10. When I look up to check again, the numbers fade into dancing cats singing about kitty litter. Is it over? So soon? The room presses in hot and heavy the way it does when you wake up from a nap in the afternoon sun.

We got one number, Young Ju, Uhmma

says in a soft voice. She pats my shoulder before standing up to go finish washing the dishes.

"One number doesn't get you any money. That was a stupid waste," Joon snaps and changes the channel.

I tilt my head down in shame, look at the worn, shaggy orange rug that was too cheap to pass up at a garage sale. I bite my nails, trying to remember all the things I wanted to buy, but the dreams are lost in the roar of gunfight on TV and clanking dishes in the kitchen.

A dollar for afternoon dreams is expensive and cheap. I sigh, draw up my knees, and pull the collar of my shirt into my mouth. But somebody has to win. Somebody gets the jackpot. Why not us? The soft cotton becomes wet with spit as I chew and think of how to pay for next week's Superlotto ticket. My foot falls asleep and I shift positions. A tiny gleam catches the corner of my eyes. I glance over.

There. Shining under the lamp, Uhmma's glass flower vase of pennies. I jerk my head away. No, never. But. My eyes skim across the ceiling, down the far wall, over to the bookshelf. There.

One hundred pennies will pull a pocket low and clank loudly on the store counter. I remember today's checkout girl giving Uhmma's chapped red hands a long look as Uhmma counted out one quarter, two dimes, five nickels, and thirty pennies. I stare at the muddy, ugly pennies and wonder. Are they worth millions?

Making Sure

Apa leads. I stay a step behind. Apa peers down at the scrap of paper in his hand and then looks up at the number on the gray stucco building. I silently read the words on the plaque, Department of Immigration and Naturalization Services.

This is it, Apa says, turning to me. I nod and follow him to the glass doors. We push past and find ourselves immediately standing in line. Metal detectors. Like at the airport. I lean to one side and watch a blue-uniformed man holding some keys while a woman passes through the empty door frame. We wait for our turn.

Once we are past the metal detectors, Apa stares at a door and a sign. He stands there trying to read the words. Trying to make some sense of where we are to go for the renewal of my green card. Apa jerks his thumb at the door and asks, What does this say?

"Authorized Personnel Only," I read.

Apa waits for me to translate.

We cannot go in there. It is only for the people who work here, I say.

Apa notices a crowd of people heading for a large waiting room to our right. He starts to follow.

Apa, I call out as I read a sign posted near some double wooden doors.

He turns around, confused.

This way, I say and point in the opposite direction.

Apa rubs the back of his neck and starts back toward me.

I lead. Apa stays a step behind.

Another line. Just to get into the room. We stand and wait our turn. At the front of the line a stooped grandma with curly white hair and eyes the color of summer grass hands us a small baby-blue ticket with a number.

"This is for the information window and they will direct you to where you need to go next," the grandma repeats like a machine. Apa opens his mouth to ask a question, but the grandma has already started to hand a ticket to the person behind us. Apa and I step out of the way into the large, windowless waiting area. Rows and rows of black chairs are filled with people sitting, slouching, reading, dozing. Some people stand and line the walls like flies on a humid summer afternoon.

At the front of the room there are five windows, but only three are open. Each window is distinguished from the others by a sign that hangs below its counter with the word "Window" and a number between one and five. Above each window there is a flashing red number announcing which person may step up next. Only one window carries the sign "Information." We find two empty seats toward the front as though that will get us to the window faster.

I lean close to Apa and study the ticket in his hand. Ninety-three.

"Fifty-five," the information lady calls out.

One by one, as the information lady calls out a number, a person or whole families stand to go ask their question. Some people take only ten seconds. Others talk and talk, making the information lady tilt her head to one side and blow her wispy bangs off her forehead. Every once in a while she picks a lint ball off her dark blue wool sweater. All the people she speaks with get another ticket to wait for one of the other windows.

"Sixty-two."

A Mexican couple dressed in matching crisp blue jeans and sweatshirts with a red Reebok logo across the chest step up to the window. The wife holds her purse with both hands and does most of the talking. The information lady is bilingual and answers back quickly in Spanish, pointing to the other window. She hands them a ticket. The husband takes the number, but the wife is still not satisfied with the answer. The two women go back and forth for a little while longer until the information lady refuses to say anything more, just keeps pointing to the other window.

The wife gives up and joins her husband, who has inched to the left to lean up against the wall. They both study the number in his hand. They look up at the blinking red number over the window they are supposed to go to next. The husband shoves his hands deep into his pockets. He walks back to their seats. The wife continues to stand by the wall, her eyes locked on the red number, her lips moving silently as though praying for a quick turnover.

Apa shifts in his seat and begins to mutter, This is going to take all day. Why do they not open up all the windows? He stands up and wanders around the waiting room, shuffling through newspapers left in empty seats. I lean my elbow on the armrest and prop my chin up with my hand. This *will* take all day. Even school is better than this.

By the time the information lady calls out our number, "Ninety-three," Apa has somehow managed to find an old *Korea Times* newspaper and is so busy reading that he does not hear her.

Apa, I think that is our number, I say, nudging his arm.

What? Apa looks up from his paper toward the information window.

Where is the number, Apa? I ask.

Here, Apa says, checking his pockets.

The information lady calls out our number again. "Ninety-three."

I know that is our number, I say and stand up. Let us go.

Apa follows after me, still searching for the lost number.

"Yes?" the information lady says.

I start to step forward, but Apa rushes in past me. He found the number. He lays the wrinkled baby-blue scrap of paper on the counter and asks our question. "We here for green card. For her." Apa points at me.

"You'll have to go to window three. Here is your number."

Apa reaches out and takes the new number.

"No, wait," I interrupt. "I have a green card. I'm supposed to renew it or something." I turn to Apa and say, Apa, can you get my green card out?

What are you doing? Apa asks me, his eyes slightly narrowed. This ahjimma has already given us a number for the next window.

Apa, please give me the green card, I say

again, a begging note cracking my voice. The information lady taps her pen against the counter. Apa pulls out his wallet and finds my card. He hands it over to the information lady instead of placing it in my outstretched hand.

The information lady looks at the numbers and words written like ant trails on the back of my card. She looks up at me. "Are you turning thirteen?" she asks.

"Yes, that's it. I'm supposed to renew my card, right?"

"Yes. Give me that number back and I'll give you a new one for window four."

I turn to Apa and say, Apa, you have to give the number back.

Apa growls low, What is going on? What are you telling this ahjimma? You better not get the wrong information. I cannot take off another day from work to come back here.

Apa, you have to give back the number, I say again. She will give us another number. When Apa squints his eyes at me, I add, For the right window.

Apa reluctantly places the baby-blue scrap of paper back on the counter. The information lady gives us another number, 36, and points to window four. We find ourselves another set of seats. Two elderly Chinese men have taken our old ones.

At window four, Apa doesn't speak, just

hands over my green card to the young black man in the same dark blue wool sweater. The man, while reading the card, says, "So, Young Ju, you're turning thirteen." He lowers the card. "Did I say your name right?"

I can't help smiling and nodding.

"Well, happy early birthday," he says with an answering nod. He slides the green card back to me. Piano fingers. He has long, lean piano fingers like what Amanda wishes she had so she could stretch her hand across one full octave.

"What we doing," Apa asks impatiently.

"Well, sir, you'll have to fill out some paperwork and get a picture taken of your daughter. Here." Piano Fingers reaches under his desk and pulls out some forms. "If you or your daughter will just read that over, it'll explain all the steps you need to take to renew Young Ju's green card."

"What more?" Apa asks. "Cannot do now. Here?"

Apa, I say, we can look at the papers at home.

Stop talking. Apa points his finger at me in warning. I am speaking with this man now.

"Sir, you can look at all the paperwork at home and then mail in the renewal fee, forms, and photograph. There's even a list of establishments that take the particular photo we need for the green card." Piano Fingers takes out another sheet from under his desk and shows Apa the list.

"I no can come back. I work every day."

"Sir, you don't need to come back. Just mail in the forms."

Apa, I plead, we can leave now. This man has given us all the forms and we can mail it in.

Yah, Apa yells at me. What did I say? I am the one who is talking now.

"Sir, you have everything you need. Once we have all the paperwork, we'll mail you Young Ju's new green card."

"You making sure," Apa says, pointing to the papers. "I no come back again. Making sure."

Ever since Apa had to go four times to clear up some mistake with Joon's Social Security number, he has become paranoid that people are trying to trick him.

"Making sure," Apa says again.

"Sir, we have a long line of people waiting."

"I waiting."

Piano Fingers looks at me.

"Please," I whisper, stepping closer to the tall counter. "Please, just look through the paperwork one more time."

Piano Fingers clasps his hands in front of his face. He presses his lips together and stares down at me and then at Apa. His eyes linger on the deep red permanent sunburn of Apa's neck from mowing lawns all day. Piano Fingers picks up the papers again. He leafs through them slowly. After he has gone through all the forms, he leans forward and addresses Apa in a clear, clipped voice. "Sir. All the necessary paperwork is right here. See? Just fill out the forms and mail them in with a check and a photograph of your daughter." Piano Fingers pushes the papers to Apa.

Apa picks them up and holds them to his face as though he is reading closely. The way Apa takes his time, licking his fingertips to separate each page from the next, makes the blood crest under my cheeks. I gaze down at my feet and take a deep breath.

"Good," Apa finally says. "I no come back. Right? No missing work again."

"No, sir, you don't have to come back."

Apa steps away from the window and turns to leave.

"Thank you," I say to Piano Fingers.

He smiles briefly, flashing me a row of white picket-fence teeth. As I turn around to leave, I hear him call out the next number, "Thirty-seven."

When we return to the car, Apa slumps in his seat and grips the green-card renewal forms with his brown callused fingers. The dark circles under his eyes gather in puffy tucks when he squints at the words. He glances up from the forms and reads the afternoon traffic for how long it will take us to get back home — maybe he can fit in a nap before leaving for his night job cleaning lawyers' offices downtown. Apa blows out his breath in a noisy sigh and turns in his seat to hand me the papers. In that moment, when the papers pass from his hands to mine, our eyes meet and I know. His will always be a face washed and dressed by sun.

Apa turns on the ignition and eases the car out of the parking space. With his eyes focused on the road, Apa says in a weary voice, Read those forms carefully. I do not want to go back to that office again. Make sure.

Reaching

I cling to the branch with one hand and lean out. The wind sings in my ears. If I could just get out a little farther, let the branch go and take one more step, I could almost touch the cloud. But I'm afraid to let go of the branch, so I continue to stretch. It's right there. Almost.

The ringing of the phone wakes me from my dream. My arms ache as though I have just fallen from the sky. I open my eyes and flop over onto my stomach, stretching out my hands, reaching under my pillow for the coolness of the sheet. I rest my chin on the pillow and look up through my window to gaze at the stars.

My dream of the cloud is not new. I have had variations of the same dream since we immigrated to America. Sometimes I fall from the tree. Sometimes I wake up before I have even finished climbing to the highest branch. Most times I am leaning out, reaching. But in every dream there are always the clouds just beyond my grasp. They float close above me in thick, solid folds of billowy white sheets. In my dream I have somehow figured out that to catch a cloud means I'll fly to heaven. Fly to the place that I have never seen but only dreamed exists. Heaven, the place I was supposed to go, but instead I ended up here.

Young Ju, Uhmma calls softly, opening my bedroom door.

I pretend I'm sleeping instead of thinking about my dream. I rub my eyes and squint against the hall light streaming into my room.

What, Uhmma? I ask.

Young Ju, Uhmma says and comes to my bed. She strokes my face with her worn hands. My skin tickles beneath her rough fingers. Her face is wet with tears.

Uhmma, what is wrong? I ask and sit up.

Uhmma bites her lip and looks away. She reaches for my hand and says quietly, Your Halmoni has passed away.

What? Halmoni is gone? I shake my head, unsure of what this means. Passed away? Dead? I have not seen Halmoni since I was four years old, so I can't be quite sure of how death takes her even farther from me.

Uhmma brushes a stray hair from my face. She whispers, Your Apa is very sad.

I sit up and move my feet from under the covers, hanging them over the edge of my bed. I lean my head against Uhmma's shoulder and gaze out the window.

We did not expect her to leave us so quickly, Uhmma says. She was always so strong. Like a horse. Uhmma sighs. We thought that she would wait for us to come back and visit.

I listen to Uhmma talk and think about the only clear memory I have of Halmoni's face. We were walking on the beach and the wind whipped Halmoni's long skirt around her legs. She bent down to adjust the hem so it did not tangle around her ankles. Then as she reached for my hand, her face turned toward mine, the last firelight rays of sun softened her wrinkles. Her face shone, polished as a beach pebble.

My other memories of Halmoni come in puzzle pieces: a hand on my back, a few notes from a bedtime song, the deep well of her lap, her voice telling me to pray. I wish I could gather all the pieces from my mind, lay them out on the floor, and fit them together. But I know there will be too many ugly gaps for any real picture to exist. A salty tear runs into my lips.

Uhmma moves her shoulder and wakes me from my thoughts. Young Ju, Uhmma says. Go to your Apa. You are the only one who loved Halmoni like your Apa did. Go to him.

Uhmma, do I have to?

Uhmma clucks her tongue. Yah. What kind

of talk is that? Your Apa is in such pain and you do not even want to comfort him? What kind of daughter are you?

I bow my head.

Uhmma puts her arm around my waist. Go ahead, Young Ju. Go to him. It will make you both feel better.

Apa sits cross-legged on the living room floor, his back against the couch. He stares out the large window by the front door. No lights have been turned on. Only the moonlight keeps him company.

Apa, I call out softy from the edge of the hallway.

His face turns toward me at the sound of my voice, but he doesn't really seem to see me.

Apa, I say again and step out from the hall.

Young Ju? Apa says. The corners of his lips turn down as though he disapproves of my being up at this hour.

Yes, Apa, I answer.

Why are you not sleeping? You have school tomorrow.

I know, Apa.

Go back to bed. Get some rest. Apa turns back to the window and sighs.

I stay where I am, gripping the shaggy strands of the carpet between my toes. We stay that way, not speaking, for what seems like years, but the clock ticks only minutes. The guttural roar of a lone car driving by the house draws my eyes to the window. I notice the moonlight on the chain-link fence, the way it turns even the ugliest pattern into a delicate, luminous web.

Apa clears his throat, and without looking away from the window, says, Halmoni was only seventy-four. Only seventy-four.

She was still young, I add.

Yes, she was.

We fall silent again. The drip from the kitchen faucet marks the passing of time. I start to grow cold in my pajamas. I take a step back, my warm bed beckoning, when I think of something to say.

Apa, are you going to go back to Korea for the funeral?

Apa shakes his head. He runs his hands through his hair, gripping his scalp, his neck. He whispers, I cannot even be at her funeral. What kind of son am I? What kind of son am I? His shoulders shake and shake.

I walk over to the couch and sit down. I remember the way Halmoni would sing me to sleep, beating the soothing rhythm of a song on the wing of my shoulder blade. I try to hum a few bars, my hand hovering over Apa's back, but the song sticks inside my throat, refusing to come out. I lower my hand and remain silent.

Apa looks up at me, the corner of his eyes tight with pain. He tells me, Halmoni was a good woman. She always tried her best to make everyone happy.

I nod.

Apa turns back around, puts his hands together as though he is praying, and holds them to his lips. He talks to himself. She would tell me not to borrow the money to fly out there. She would tell me to use it on more important things. Apa starts to cry again, pounding his fists into his forehead. She would tell me that. She would. She would. Would she not?

Apa. Apa. I say it over and over again, trying to call him back to himself. Who is this man crying like an abandoned child? This is not my Apa who growls instead of talks. My eyes search out the window. A small wisp of cloud hovers in the sky wearing the moonlight like a silver dress.

I imagine somewhere, in that sky, Halmoni is in heaven, bowing and greeting Harabugi and Jesus. There, her back will never be tired, and she'll fly with the angels and not say once, Slow down. This was always her dream. To be up there. In heaven. I am still here, reaching.

Apa, I say and rest my hand on his shoulder. Halmoni is already in heaven. She does not need you to fly to Korea to see her. She can see you.

Apa bows his head. He reaches back and holds my hand.

My Best Is Always Not Enough

A rectangle. Picture frame. Doorway. Apa sits at his card table desk, both elbows on the surface. He holds a piece of paper up to his face, moving his lips, feeling his way among the foreign words. He puts the paper back down and cups his chin with one hand; the other hand punches numbers into a calculator. The small green desk lamp on the far corner of his table throws the shadows of his face deeper, longer. Into the night.

A noise in the kitchen startles me from my reading and I check the clock. Past midnight already. I stretch in my chair and yawn. I wonder if it is Uhmma in the kitchen. She should be sleeping. Sunday is the only day she can fit in a full night's rest. I glance at my notes again. Tomorrow's history exam has me worried, but there is nothing more I can do so late at night. I'll check on Uhmma and then get some sleep.

I walk down the hallway, my fingers lightly following the wall, my eyes fixed on a tiny light coming from the kitchen. My step falters when I hear Uhmma's voice.

Where were you? Uhmma asks.

That is not your concern, Apa slurs.

You have an early-morning gardening job tomorrow and you get drunk the night before. What kind of responsible man are you?

I told you, woman, Apa growls low. That is not your concern.

I hear Apa cursing loudly as he steps into the living room. I take a few steps back, turn, and flee quietly to my room. Safely behind my door, my heart finally slows.

The crashing is loud and strong. I plug my ears but can still hear Apa's loud yelling. Who do you think you are? Questioning me. *Slap.*

Stop it, I say to myself. Go out there and stop it. But I do nothing. Say nothing. Only listen to the walls like a shameful mouse.

Yuhboh, Uhmma cries.

You think I am worthless. I see it in your eyes. A son who does not even go to his own uhmma's funeral. A husband who does not provide you with enough. You always want more. But there is nothing. Look, we have nothing. My best is always not enough. Get away from me. You are strangling me to death with your hopes.

Uhmma's sharp cry shatters the air.

The front door slams. In the distance, the

station wagon sputters to life, then fades into the night.

I tiptoe out into the hallway again. Uhmma sits on the floor, crying softly in the dark living room. I walk over and kneel down, sit silent as a shadow by her side.

Uhmma clutches something close to her chest and rocks back and forth in rhythm to her sobs. When Uhmma's shoulders cannot shake anymore, when her throat finally opens and her breathing steadies, I touch her shoulder and say, Uhmma.

Go to sleep, Young Ju, Uhmma says with a sigh, trying to stand. Aigoo.

I grab Uhmma's arm and help her onto the couch. When I turn on the lamp, Uhmma squints and turns her face away from the light. But not before I see her swollen eye.

The coffee table is overturned, Korean newspaper strewn all over the carpet. The smell of Apa's alcohol breath soaks the air. I pick up a broken picture frame, the photo of our family at the airport in Korea slightly skewed, and set it on the couch. In the kitchen, I find an old plastic bag and fill it with some ice.

Here, Uhmma, I say and offer her the bag of ice. Uhmma takes it from me, presses it to her eye, and grimaces. I stand hovering above her, unsure of what to do, what to say, how I can help. On her lap, I notice the checkbook. Uhmma sees me staring and pushes the checkbook under her leg, out of sight.

Young Ju, go to sleep, Uhmma says.

But Uhmma, I protest.

Please, Young Ju, Uhmma begs.

I press my lips together, give Uhmma a few seconds to change her mind.

Do not speak of this to anyone, Uhmma says. Not even Gomo. Now go to sleep.

I walk back to my bedroom.

A rectangle. Picture frame. Doorway. Uhmma sits at Apa's card table desk, both elbows on the surface. She holds the checkbook up to her face, moving her lips, feeling her way among the numbers. She puts the checkbook down and cups her chin with one hand; the other hand punches numbers into a calculator. While she checks the numbers on the calculator against the numbers in the checkbook, Uhmma absentmindedly rubs her thumb back and forth. Back and forth over the unfamiliar nakedness of her ring finger. The small green desk lamp on the far corner of the table throws the shadows of her face deeper, longer. Into the night.

The Power of Prayer

Today we are going to church, Uhmma announces.

Joon and I look up from our breakfast bowls of rice and seaweed soup.

Church? I ask.

Uhmma sits down with her bowl of soup and nods. She says, I met the minister while I was shopping at the Korean market.

Wait, he was not one of those men who stand outside all day? I ask.

He does not stay there the whole day, Uhmma says, taking a sip of her soup.

I close my eyes. This is the man who wears his pants hitched up to his chin and a white button-down shirt. Every Friday and Saturday he stands outside with his stack of writings about what prayer and God can do to change your life. I have seen him jump over bushes to make sure someone did not leave the store without a little stapled booklet. I hate the way he smiles so big you can see his pasty pink gums.

Uhmma puts down her spoon and says, Grace Church is just starting and the minister is a very welcoming and understanding man. Uhmma picks up her spoon and takes a sip of her soup. We need some prayer in our lives, she adds.

Joon pretends he has not heard any of it. He keeps his head down and shoves more soup into his mouth.

What about Apa? I ask. Will Apa go to church too?

Uhmma shakes her head, her eyes on her soup.

I look down the hall toward the bedroom where Apa is still sleeping. More and more, instead of going to his gardening job on Sundays, he stays home drinking beer and watching TV. Joon and I hide in our rooms reading. It's better to stay out of his sight.

All the way to church, Joon sits in the back seat with his arms crossed. Every once in a while he sighs so loud it sounds like he's trying to blow the station wagon off course. Uhmma doesn't even check the rear-view mirror. She knows that Joon, like Apa, can cast a scowl so long it shadows his entire face.

I sit in the front seat staring out the window, thinking about the time that Halmoni taught me to pray. Her hands folded on top of mine, her whispered words. Now that I'm older, I don't really believe there is someone listening to me. But Uhmma must still believe. I glance at her. Uhmma gently pats the back of her head, making sure all the strands of her braided hair are in place. When she catches me staring, she blushes and puts her hand back on the steering wheel.

Grace Church is nothing but a basement rented from the bigger church with white people upstairs. Every once in a while you can hear everyone standing up for a song. Feet shuffle so loud the ceiling sounds ready to rain. The main part of the basement is lined with hard brown foldout chairs already filled with people. Up at the front of the room a man with slicked-down hair stands at a podium surrounded by two stands of yellow and white flowers. He busily sets out some books and prepares himself for the sermon. I strain my neck to see if it's the same man who jumps over the bushes. The sharp click of high-heeled shoes rings out behind us. A woman with her hair cut short as a boy's, but lips covered in bright pink lipstick to match the pink scarf at her throat, waves to us.

Ahn-young-ha-say-yo, she says and bows. I am the minister's wife, Mrs. Kim.

Ahn-young-ha-say-yo, Uhmma says and bows back. I am Mrs. Park and these are my children, Park Young Ju and Park Joon Ho. Uhmma pushes us forward.

Ahn-young-ha-say-yo, I say and bow.

Joon mumbles something that sounds close to the formal greeting, but he does not bow. Uhmma gives Joon a hard look and then starts to pat her cheek nervously.

Mrs. Park, the minister's wife says, we are delighted that you could join us on such a fine Sunday morning. The Lord has truly blessed us today, amen.

Amen, Uhmma says shyly.

The minister's wife turns to us. Young Ju and Joon Ho, you must be very excited to meet the other children and the youth minister, Mr Shin. She says to Uhmma, He is a most fine speaker. They will enjoy Sunday school.

We follow Mrs. Kim to a small, square room at the back of the basement. A thin man who looks young enough to be a college student leans against a desk talking in a loud, nasal voice. Uhmma bumps me forward and then waves good-bye when I turn around to give her a dirty look. They quietly close the door behind them and leave Joon and me standing there.

I scan the room, trying to find a place to sit, and notice the tall file cabinets in the corner, the phone on the desk. This room looks more like an office than a classroom. In the far back corner, at the edge of the rug, there is some space. I pull on Joon's shirt and we make our way next to two girls with the same shoulder-length black hair. They scoot over to give us more room. Joon and I sit cross-legged on the floor.

For an hour Mr. Shin uses Korean and English examples to talk about the compassion of God. Joon immediately gets bored and begins to unravel the edge of the rug. Though I try to pay attention, my eyes keep wandering over to the two girls sitting directly in front of me. They look about eleven, maybe twelve. Their matching yellow shirts and brown jumpers, not to mention the same haircut and daisy barrettes, make them look like twins. I check their hair for split ends.

When my legs begin to tingle from sitting still too long, I tap one of the twins and ask for directions to the bathroom. She whispers, "It's out in the big hall, by the front door."

I tiptoe quietly across the large room. Uhmma sits by herself in the back row. Her head is bowed, her back rounded, shoulders slumped. For a moment, I stop walking and stare at her small, huddled form. The chorus up front sings a slow song filled with high notes that reach impossibly for the sky. Uhmma prays, though everyone else around her sings.

After the adult service ends, we meet Uhmma in the fellowship hall. Joon stands in front of the refreshment table greedily piling his square napkin with doughnuts. Uhmma walks around with the minister's wife, bowing to everyone she meets. After she makes it all the way around the room, she comes back to Joon and me.

Time to go home, Uhmma says, her face flushed pink at the top of her cheeks. She delicately tucks some stray hairs behind her ear.

Joon grabs another doughnut as we leave.

On the car ride home, Uhmma glances at me and asks, Did you like Sunday school?

I shrug.

Did you like it, Joon Ho?

The sermon was boring, Joon replies from the back. But the doughnuts were good.

Our answers do not seem to bother Uhmma. She simply says that church will get better once we know more people. Then she begins to hum. Not a song really, just a pattern of notes tied together like popcorn on string. Uhmma hums all the way past the exit to our house.

Uhmma, I remind her, you missed the exit.

I know, Uhmma says. We are not going home yet. I feel like going to the beach.

Hardly anyone goes to the beach on a breezy winter day except a few walkers. The wind whips our hair around our faces, but the bright sun keeps us warm, almost hot. Joon runs ahead, his shoes and socks already pulled off and dangling from his hands. He slip-slides through the sand, heading for the water's edge. Uhmma and I remove our shoes and step off the sidewalk. A dog in the distance barks at a seagull that has gotten too close.

Uhmma holds her high heels in one hand, her stocking feet buried in the sand. The other hand shields her eyes as she takes in the horizon. Today, Uhmma says, I feel like I can take in a full breath of air.

I nod and swirl my feet through the rough grains, enjoying the gritty tickling at the bottom of my feet.

Uhmma begins to sing the song from church, the one that reached impossibly for the sky. I listen to Uhmma sing. Her voice carries all the high notes.

Becoming Too American

It is Amanda's first party. A beach birthday party. With boys. I can't go. Uhmma and Apa do not like it that my best friend is an American, a girl who might influence me in the wrong ways. Fast American ways. Supposedly, American girls do not study, they are boy-crazy, and they do not think of anyone but themselves. Uhmma and Apa do not want me to end up like them.

But Uhmma, I beg, following her down the hall to the kitchen. It is her birthday.

No, Young Ju. You can see her at school and give her your gift then, but you do not need to go to the beach with her.

Why? I ask and slam my body into a chair. Why, Uhmma? What is so wrong with going to the beach?

Always why with you. Do not let your Apa hear those kinds of words. Already he has been complaining that you ask too many questions. Aigoo, Young Ju, we will go to the beach another time, Uhmma says. She pulls some scallions out of the refrigerator and rinses them off in the sink.

That is not the same, I cry. Amanda needs me at the party. I am her best friend!

As Uhmma carries the scallions to the cutting board near the stove, she gives me a narrow-eyed glance. This is a sore subject.

I change my tactics. Uhmma, Amanda has been so nice to me. When I missed school from that cold, she gave me all her notes from class.

That is nice, Uhmma says and chops the scallions in half.

And when it was my birthday she got me this necklace, I say and pull out from under my shirt collar my half of the FRIENDS FOREVER heart necklace.

Uhmma presses her lips together but does not look in my direction. She lines up the halves of the scallions and starts to chop. Fine slivers of green and white circles cover the cutting board.

I slump in my seat and say, And when I did not have any lunch money, she let me borrow some from her.

What! Uhmma stops chopping in mid-motion, knife raised in the air.

Nothing, I quickly say.

What did you say, Young Ju? Uhmma waves the knife in the air.

I scratch my cheek, look up at the ceiling, sigh. When I did not have any lunch money

136

and we ran out of bread last week, Amanda let me borrow some money.

Young Ju, how could you do this? Uhmma cries, putting down the knife. You took money from Ah-man-dah? Uhmma asks.

Yes, I say. She is my friend and she said I could borrow it.

Now you are obligated to her. Uhmma leans her hip against the counter.

I am not obligated to her, Uhmma. I am going to pay her back.

Young Ju, have I not taught you never to take from others? Do not make yourself obligated to another person.

Uhmma, she is my friend. I stand up and wave my arms in the air. This is America. In America it is fine to borrow money from friends.

Stop that, Uhmma says. We are Korean. Do not forget.

I sit back down. Korean. Then why did we move to America?

You can go to the party, Uhmma says.

I'm so stunned I'm not sure I heard correctly. Did she say I could go?

What? I ask.

You must fulfill your obligation for inconveniencing her. Also, you will pay her back the money you borrowed. Uhmma shakes her head. Have I not taught you anything? After this, do not take anything from her. Understand?

Yes, Uhmma. I jump out of my chair to get ready for the party before she has a chance to change her mind.

As Uhmma drives toward the pier, I can see a group of kids from school in the far distance.

I turn to Uhmma. Stop, Uhmma. You can drop me off here.

The station wagon's brakes groan and then squeal in a high-pitched scream as Uhmma comes to a stop near the curb.

Uhmma squints at the kids. Are those not your friends over there?

I turn my head away from her and look out my window at the long stretch of sand. I lie softly, That is another group. You can drop me off here and I will look around for Amanda. She said they would be near the pier.

Are you sure you will be able to find them? Uhmma worries.

I open the car door and toss back, Do not worry, Uhmma, I know where to find them. Remember that Amanda is going to drop me off at home so you do not have to come back and get me.

Yes, I will remember, Uhmma says.

I step out of the car and wave good-bye. Uhmma leans across the passenger seat, giving me a finger shake. Young Ju, do not forget to give Ah-man-dah the money you borrowed. Be a polite girl and help her parents with the party.

I hold the door, ready to slam it shut. Yes, Uhmma, I say, waving again. "Bye."

Uhmma waves back. Have a nice time, Young Ju.

I slam the door and walk away. The station wagon sputters as Uhmma presses on the gas pedal. I know without turning around that there are dark clouds of smoke streaming from the muffler.

Amanda and her parents do not know where I live. We have always hung out at Amanda's house because I lied and said Uhmma and Apa owned a restaurant that kept them working long hours so there was usually no one home. Mr. Doyle, Amanda's father, drives slowly, waiting for my instructions.

"Just up that hill," I say and point to a wide street lined with well-kept lawns and flower-beds. "There's my house." I nod my head at a two-story gray stucco bungalow on the corner. The heavy wooden front doors gleam under the entrance light.

"Well, here you go, Young," Amanda's dad says as he eases the car in front of my pretend house.

"I'm really glad you got to come, Young," Amanda says and bumps her shoulder against mine.

"Happy birthday, Amanda." I give her a quick hug. I gather up my towel and goody bag, then lean forward to thank Amanda's parents. "Thank you for the ride, Mr. and Mrs. Doyle."

Mrs. Doyle turns in her seat and reaches back to hold my hand. "No problem, Young. It was wonderful to have you at the party. Have a good night."

"See ya at school on Monday, Young," Amanda says.

"See ya," I call back and get out of the car. I stand at the top of the driveway and wave, hoping Amanda and her parents will drive away. But the Doyles peer out at me from their windows, their various shades of blond hair gleaming under the small light inside their car. They are waiting for me to go inside, making sure I get in safely. Amanda waves to me. I wave back and turn around. After a deep breath and a wish with all of my body that no one is in the yard, I carefully lift the latch to the door in the tall wooden fence. Quietly I walk through and close the door behind me. The Doyles' car starts up. I wait in the strange darkness of my make-believe yard, listening for the silence that will allow me to escape to where I belong.

As I walk back down the hill, I notice that the air seems fresher up here. Like it is out in the country or something. Even the faint smell of fertilizer seems clean. The bright moonlight makes everything glow more fiercely. The lawns, mowed smooth and flat as a new-made bed, gleam a strange, poisonous green. I kneel down and run my fingers through the cool blades to make sure they really exist. I'm glad we buried Harry up here. I take a deep breath of air and hold it in my lungs for as long as I can.

In my neighborhood, instead of lawns there are fields of concrete and asphalt. It is rare to see grass, and even then it's usually dead. The crisscross metal fence around the apartment we rent sags in the middle from the weather, from the weight of too many kids leaning up against it, from the neglect of the owner. I walk up the oil-stained driveway and head inside.

Uhmma, I call out as I step through the front door, I am back.

Uhmma pokes her head out from the kitchen. She smiles, asking, Did you have a good time?

Yes.

Dinner will be ready in a few minutes. Your Apa should be home by then.

I nod and head to my room.

After the chatter of the Doyles, the quiet at the dinner table sounds strange to my ears. I eat my rice and wonder why my parents can't speak or joke with the ease of Mr. and Mrs. Doyle. Why can't Apa barbecue and ask Uhmma if she needs any help? Or Uhmma tease Apa and then lightly kiss him on the cheek to make sure he knows she was only kidding?

Apa picks up his beer, takes a long sip. He puts the beer back down, and without looking at Uhmma, says, Tomorrow I need the car.

Uhmma sips her tea. But Yuhboh, Uhmma says, tomorrow we have church. Do you need the car for a job?

Apa sighs angrily and says, You can miss church for one day. He shoves some rice into his mouth.

I listen to their conversation, keeping my head lowered, pretending to eat my food.

Uhmma asks carefully, If it is not for a job, could you not wait until after we get back?

Apa narrows his eyes and picks up some kimchee with his chopsticks. Before putting it in his mouth, he growls, What good is God going to do? Miss church.

Uhmma does not respond. She keeps her eyes on her tea.

Apa, I call out, suddenly remembering, I

have chorus practice tomorrow.

Apa slowly chews his kimchee.

I cannot miss chorus practice because we are getting ready for the Easter pageant, I insist.

Be quiet and finish your rice, Apa says. He takes another long sip of his beer.

Before I can stop my tongue, I question Apa as though I'm in school or with Amanda. I ask, Why do you need the car?

The skin around Uhmma's eyes wrinkles in concern, her lips gather together in a knot. The slight shake of her head warns me to stop. But it is too late.

Apa grips his beer. His eyes narrow and a smooth, tight voice snakes out, It is always why with you. Stand up, Apa orders.

I slowly push back my chair and stand in my place by the table.

Come here, Apa says.

I take small, careful steps, avoiding any glances at Uhmma or Joon. I stop when I see Apa's gold-toe socks.

You, Apa shouts and hits the side of my head with his knuckles, *will never question me.*

Arrows of pain shoot through my head, making me squint. Find a corner of the carpet. Concentrate. Float away.

Apa yells, Asking for an explanation! Always getting your own way! You have been running around with that American girl for too long. You are not allowed to see her anymore. She is a bad influence.

I can't see Amanda? My only friend. The only person who lets me ask questions and be someone other than a good Korean daughter. The thought of not seeing Amanda makes me so angry I can barely hold on to my corner of the carpet.

You are becoming too American. That girl is worthless, Apa says.

No, I argue quietly. She is not.

Slam.

The carpet feels soft and cool against my throbbing cheek. I clutch the strands.

Do not get up, Apa says, standing over me. Do not get up until you know how to be a Korean girl again.

Punishment

The voices start early Saturday morning. Gomo's and Uncle Tim's voices are quiet and soft. Uhmma's cry rises high, then dips down fast when someone says, Shhhh. The only voice missing is Apa's. Where is he, I wonder and press my ear to my bedroom door, afraid to peek out. I can hear Gomo saying sharp and fast, I am ashamed of you.

Uhmma whimpers, Aigoo. Aigoo chamneh. Yuhboh, how could you do this? How could you?

Unde Tim says, Do not worry. Do not worry.

I picture Uncle Tim patting Uhmma on the back, his shoulders drooping forward so he won't seem so tall.

It is his first offense, Uncle Tim says. Do not worry. I will find you a good lawyer.

This is the first and last time, Gomo says quickly, her voice cracking from the effort of keeping her tone at a whisper. What an embarrassment you have become.

Uhmma cries louder, How could this have happened? Aigoo.

You must change, Gomo says. What kind of example are you setting for your children? Getting arrested for drunk driving. You are acting like a common hoodlum.

"Honey, that's enough," Uncle Tim says.

"I help him enough," Gomo says.

"Come on. Let him get some rest."

Gomo announces, We are leaving. Tomorrow, Byung Ho, we will have a long talk.

I can't hear Apa's answer if he spoke at all. The front door clicks shut and then I hear footsteps rustle to Uhmma and Apa's bedroom door.

The clatter of Uhmma in the kitchen finally draws me out of my room. I walk into the hallway and see Uhmma standing at her usual spot in front of the stove. The only sign of Apa is the closed bedroom door.

As we are eating breakfast, Uhmma warns Joon and me to remain quiet today, maybe go to the park so Apa can rest. There is no mention of why Apa is home this morning. I wonder if he will lose his cleaning job like some of the gardening jobs. While I clear the breakfast dishes, Uhmma takes her Bible down from a shelf and opens it to a certain page. She counts out the money she has managed to save for emergencies. I watch her but don't ask any questions. After she leaves for the restaurant, I walk quietly around the house looking for anything to prove that the distant voices, which seem more and more like a dream, were real.

The next morning Apa comes out of the bedroom for the first time since he came home yesterday morning. Uhmma, Joon, and I are eating breakfast before going to church. Apa picks up the Korean newspaper and sits down on the couch. A dark shadow covers his upper lip, and his sweat suit is rumpled. The phone rings. Uhmma stands to pick it up.

Good morning, Gomo, Uhmma says. Yes, he is out of bed.

Apa lowers his paper and squints narrowly at Uhmma.

You are coming over, Gomo?

Wait, Apa says and glances over at Joon and me. Tell her I am getting ready for church.

Joon bumps my arm with his elbow. I keep staring at my rice.

Gomo, Uhmma says after a pause, Young Ju's Apa is getting ready for church right now. Yes, I agree. Church will be good for him.

Apa raises his newspaper and begins to read again.

Yes, he will call you when we come home. Good-bye. Uhmma hangs up but remains standing with her hand over the phone. Uhmma looks over at Apa. Do not make me a liar, Yuhboh.

Apa does not put down the paper.

I will not lie for you. I will call Gomo back. I will tell her.

Apa throws down his paper with an angry hiss and walks back to the bedroom.

Uhmma drives to church. Apa sits in the passenger seat, shaven and clean, wearing a white shirt and the only tie he owns, the one he wore on the plane from Korea. The red diagonal strips are thick as a barbershop's pole. Apa's hair is wet and slicked down, his cowlick forced to lie still. Apa stares straight out the window the entire way.

At church, Pastor Kim is speaking with another family, but when he sees Uhmma walk in with Apa, his chin lifts. He bows quickly to the other family and hurries over to us.

Ahn-young-ha-say-yo, Mr. Park, he says, bowing and shaking Apa's hand. We are very happy to have you with us today. Your wife has become a most valued member of our congregation. And your children are so nice.

Apa nods, but his eyes shift around the room, flitting from person to person, family to family. Uhmma keeps her head bowed, hands folded together. Joon hops from foot to foot, impatient to run off down the hall toward the Sunday school room where he knows that some of his friends are already playing a game of Sorry before Mr. Shin's sermon. I stand next to Uhmma, my hands folded, and wait to be excused.

Pastor Kim turns to us. He gives Joon a pat on the shoulder and says, My goodness, Joon, how you are growing. You are almost as tall as I am.

Joon shoves his hands into his pocket. Uhmma nudges him and Joon answers, Yes.

Pastor Kim smiles and gestures as though announcing me on stage. He tells my parents, Young Ju is looking very grown up. More and more like a demure young lady.

My toes curl inside my shoes at the mention of becoming a young lady. My shoulders hunch slightly forward to cover any signs of my developing young-lady body.

Apa stands through all of this, his back stiff, a layer of sweat already glistening on his upper lip.

Pastor Kim continues, Your wife has been —

Apa interrupts before Pastor Kim can finish with his compliments. Thank you for your words, he says abruptly and leads Uhmma away to the back row of chairs. Pastor Kim remains in his spot, a confused look on his face.

Joon immediately takes off for the Sunday school room. I follow slowly behind him after one last backward glance at Uhmma and Apa. They sit side by side in the last row. Uhmma has not sat in the back since the first day we came to church. Usually she sits in the front. Apa's cowlick is at last awake. He tries to smooth it down. Uhmma discreetly wets her fingers with some spit and reaches up, pressing the lock of hair back down. It stays in place. At least for now.

After the service while Uhmma helps set out doughnuts and coffee, Apa stands in the corner of the fellowship hall, away from everyone else, smoking a cigarette. When it looks as though someone might approach him, Apa slyly moves away to another corner of the room, pretends to become interested in his crumpled program.

On the drive home, Uhmma talks about how Pastor Kim wants her to join the chorus, they need more sopranos. Uhmma asks Apa if he liked the sermon. Apa remains silent. Uhmma grips the steering wheel tighter and tighter, the outlines of her knuckles growing sharp. Joon looks out of his window and I look out of mine. We all stay silent for the rest of the ride home.

Apa yanks off his tie as soon as we step inside the house and starts down the hallway for the bedroom. Uhmma calls to his retreating back, Yuhboh, remember to call Gomo.

Apa slams the bedroom door behind him.

Uhmma sighs and sits down on the couch,

absentmindedly tucking in the corners of the yellow sheet that covers the cushions. She takes off her high heels and rubs her ankles while staring out the front window.

Young Ju and Joon Ho, Uhmma calls, find something to eat. I am too tired to cook.

Joon and I search the cupboards for a snack.

Apa walks out of the bedroom changed into jeans and an old button-down shirt. He heads for the front door.

Yuhboh, wait. Uhmma stands up. Where are you going? You are not allowed to drive.

I do not care. I have had enough punishment for today, Apa says without turning around.

Yuhboh, please, you might get caught. Please, Uhmma begs, reaching for his arm. When will you be back? What if the lawyer calls?

Apa jerks his arm away from Uhmma and leaves. He does not return for three days. Uhmma does not sleep, circles of worry rimming her eyes. Waiting.

Daughter

The bleachers of the gymnasium are filled with parents. Some fathers wear suits and ties, having come right from work. Others wear dark pants and short-sleeved shirts with collars and miniature alligators, tigers, or men riding horses embroidered on their breast pocket. Most of the mothers have dresses on and their faces are glossy with makeup. It's strange to see the gym filled with parents instead of kids running around in their gray and purple P.E. uniforms. But the awards ceremony needed a big place. There's just enough room for all the parents who have students in honors classes. If they gave awards to people in the regular classes, the gym wouldn't hold everyone. They would need a whole football field for all those parents. And the parents would not be dressed in such nice clothes.

My own sky-blue dress is tight around the shoulders and back, but long enough that it still looks like it fits. Uhmma lowered the hem a few months ago. Only if you look real close can you see the faded line from where the hem used to be.

I sit with Amanda and her parents even though Apa has forbidden me to see her. He will never know, and Uhmma does not mind if I see Amanda at school. Mr. and Mrs. Doyle ask why I haven't been around lately. I smile awkwardly and give them the same excuse I give Amanda, "I have a lot of homework." Amanda rolls her eyes and complains I study way too much. By the time the principal steps up to the podium to begin the awards ceremony, my entire face has flamed red from my lies.

Amanda receives an award for English. When her name is announced and she stands up to accept the certificate, Mr. Doyle runs up ahead of her, snapping pictures as though she is a runway model. The flashes make Amanda falter in mid-step. She waves her father away and everyone in the crowd chuckles like they know how she feels. Amanda shakes the principal's hand, then gets a hug and a certificate from Mrs. Connor, our English teacher. Amanda walks quickly back to her seat. Mrs. Doyle claps and claps until the gym grows quiet again and the boom of her hands rings out.

After all the department awards have been handed out, they go to the GPA awards. One person in every class with the highest grade point average receives a certificate.

"The ninth-grade GPA award goes to Yungpark."

At first I am not sure if they called me because the name sounds so garbled, but when Amanda gives me a nudge, I stand up. Amanda and her parents clap loudly as I walk to the front to shake the principal's hand. He hands me the certificate, and for a second I am lost in the reflection of the shiny gold stamp.

After the ceremony ends, Mr. and Mrs. Doyle offer to give me a lift home. I panic and blurt out the truth: "That's okay, I can take the bus."

Mrs. Doyle frowns. "Now do you think that's safe, Young? Is that how you got here? Couldn't your parents —"

"Actually, Mrs. Doyle," I break in, "if you could give me a lift to the library, I have to finish up some of my research for the history final."

Amanda raises one eyebrow. She knows I'm almost done.

"It's pretty late, Young. Are you sure you want to go to the library? We can drop you at your house," Mrs. Doyle says.

"The library closes late tonight and I'd rather get the research over with."

"Linda, come on," Mr. Doyle says to his

wife. "Young knows what she's doing. Look at that certificate in her hand. She didn't earn that by picking her nose."

"Daaad!" Amanda groans and grabs my arm, leading me to the door of the gym.

On the car ride to the library, Mr. Doyle begins to sing along to a song on the radio. Amanda complains that he is embarrassing her in front of her friend. Mr. Doyle looks back at me in the rear-view mirror and winks. I smile even though I know Amanda thinks her parents are way too dorky. She is always saying she can't take them anywhere.

A few blocks before the library, a line of cars are stopped on the street. Up ahead, the blue and red lights of two police cars flash in the night. Mrs. Doyle leans to one side to see what the problem is. "I wonder what happened?" she worries. The cars slowly inch forward.

As we near the police cars, Mr. Doyle starts to nod as though he understands what is going on. He turns in his seat to look at us and explains, "They're just doing one of those sobriety checks."

"You mean for drunk driving?" Amanda asks.

Mr. Doyle nods and turns back around.

My chest tightens in anticipation even though I know Mr. Doyle has not been drinking. I think about Apa and how he was arrested. For some crazy reason, I begin to worry that maybe they'll recognize me. See me as the daughter of the man they arrested. Or worse, what if Apa is pulled to the side?

The police officer beams his flashlight into the car, making me squint for a second.

"Hello, Officer," Mr. Doyle says.

"Sir, where are you coming from tonight?"

Mr. Doyle jerks his thumb toward the back seat. "Officer, I'm carrying two of the smartest kids at Wagner High School."

The officer peers back at us. "That so," he says, smiling.

Mr. Doyle waves Amanda's certificate in the air. "My daughter won an award for English and her friend got the highest GPA in the ninth grade," Mr. Doyle brags.

"That's fine work. Fine work," the officer says. He waves his flashlight forward and says quickly, "Be careful on the roads, we have a lot of end-of-the-school-year and graduation parties going on."

"Sure thing, Officer," Mr. Doyle says and drives forward.

Only after the car rounds the corner do I finally let myself breathe. That was so easy. Mr. Doyle even made the guy smile. In my neighborhood, the police never get out of their cars unless it is to arrest someone or harass them with questions. Usually they cruise the streets slowly, their eyes hard and heavy with mistrust. I never thought they could actually care about other people.

After the library closes, I walk to the apartment and stay up late into the night, waiting for Uhmma to come home so I can show her the award. Uhmma holds the certificate in her hands, tilting it back and forth so the light will catch the gold medal stamp.

You were number one in your class? Uhmma asks and holds up her thumb.

Number one, Uhmma, I say and hold up my pointer finger.

Uhmma studies the certificate again. Here, she says, pointing. That is your name.

Yes.

I am very proud of you, Young Ju, Uhmma says. She picks up my hand and gives it a squeeze. Tell me, she says. Tell me about the ceremony. Did they clap very loud?

I nod.

Did Amanda and her parents stand when you went up?

I wrinkle my brow, trying to remember, and nod again.

My goodness, Uhmma says smiling. A special ceremony to honor you.

No, Uhmma, I groan. There were many

people who received awards. Amanda got one for English.

Yes, that is very nice. But that was not for being number one in the class. English is just one subject.

Yes, but it is still a good award.

Tell me what else happened. Did you have to make a speech?

No.

Did you bow?

No, Uhmma. It is not like that. I only shook the principal's hand.

Good. He is a very important man. Do you think we should send him a gift?

No, Uhmma, I groan again.

Young Ju, Uhmma says and gazes steadily into my eyes. I am very sorry I could not be there for your important night. She shakes her head and laments, To think of all those people there to honor you, and your own parents could not take a night off from their jobs. Aigoo, Young Ju. What kind of parents do you have? Your Apa will be so proud of you.

I bow my head, ashamed to remember how scared I was that the police would recognize me or that I might see Apa pulled over. I ask Uhmma, Should we try to wait up for Apa?

Uhmma frowns at the clock and then shakes her head. She says, I will leave it in a place where he will see it.

Uhmma places my certificate in the middle of the coffee table, next to the *Korea Times* newspaper. It stays there the whole night, untouched. The next morning, Uhmma tries to explain that Apa must have slept downtown in his car because he was so tired. He had to get up early to take care of a lawn down there anyway.

When Apa finally does come home, he covers the entire coffee table with his newspaper. Underneath the scattered sheets, the certificate lies tossed aside like a useless piece of mail. I push away the newspaper and pick up my award. Mr Doyle's voice, bragging to the police officer that Amanda and I are two of the smartest kids at Wagner, rings in my head. If only I were his daughter, I think and crush the corner of the award. It's only a piece of paper.

I look down at my name and begin to crumple the entire certificate, but a tiny black smudge catches my eye. For some reason, before I can think, I lift the certificate to my nose. Ammonia and bleach. An ache deep and wide as the sea threatens to drown my heart.

Revealing Forms

Sunday morning I walk out of my room and Uhmma is already in the kitchen, standing with her back to me, cleaning the counter. "Uhmma," I call as I walk down the hallway, not because I need something but simply to say I am awake.

But today, instead of her usual greeting, Did you sleep well, Uhmma's back stiffens and she quickly puts something into a brown paper bag she is holding at her side. Without turning to face me, Uhmma tells me over her shoulder, Hurry up and take a shower. We are late for church.

I walk into the living room, wondering how we could be late when it is still only seven o'clock and church does not start for another two hours. I sit down on the couch, ready to turn on the television, when I notice a strange odor in the air. Along with the smell of stale cigarettes and lingering garlic and fish from last night's dinner, there's something else. Like air freshener at a gas station bathroom. Country flowers or Tea Rose. I sniff the strange odor and look around the room. Everything looks the same.

I sniff the air again, wondering if Uhmma got up early to clean the house, which would not be unusual. But this is not the smell of Comet or Windex.

Young Ju, Uhmma calls from the kitchen. I told you to take a shower. Go now.

Uhmma, I say, wanting to ask her about the smell.

Now, Young Ju. I do not want to hear your whys, Uhmma insists. Go right now.

After my shower, I knock on Joon's door. There is no answer. I walk in anyway. Joon usually hides in his room until someone drags him out of bed.

"Go away," Joon croaks from under the pillow.

"Joon," I whisper. "Something's wrong."

"What's new."

"Joon!" I shake his shoulders, try to lift the pillow off his face.

"Knock it off, Uhn-nee," Joon cries and holds the pillow tightly in place.

I give a hard yank and the pillow is mine. Joon sits up. "Uhn-nee, what do you want?"

"Something's wrong," I say again.

"What are you talking about?" Joon grabs the pillow out of my hands and falls back on it, one arm tucked under his head.

"I don't know what it is. Just something

161

smells funny in the living room."

Joon rolls his eyes, but the way his nostrils flare and stay flared, the way they get after a lecture and a few cuffs on the head or a kick in the stomach from Apa, I know he is listening.

"So what," Joon says and rolls over. "You're probably smelling your own stinkiness."

"Joon, I'm being serious. It was a weird smell."

"Well, what was it then?"

I try to remember the odor, the edge in the air. I search his room for something that might help me put a name to this thing. I bite the inside of my cheek. "I don't know."

"Great. You got wigged out by a smell?"

"It wasn't just that," I insist. I don't tell him it was the way the smell made the back of my neck tense up.

"Uhn-nee, forget it. Uhmma was probably cleaning the house. You know how she is in the morning."

"You think so?" My hands suddenly feel cold and stiff. I sit on them so that the backs of my thighs will keep them warm.

Joon starts to snore and pretends he is going back to sleep. I yank the pillow from under his head and tell him, "Uhmma wants us to get ready for church."

Joon groans.

Uhmma is gone from the kitchen when I walk out of Joon's room. I circle through the living room again, sniffing the air, wondering at the strange odor that does not belong in this house. In the kitchen, I lift up the lid from the soup pot and check to see what's for breakfast. Empty. I put the lid back down and lean against the counter. No breakfast? Uhmma always has breakfast ready. My mouth begins to water, not from hunger, but from the familiar nervousness that makes my stomach throw up all of its contents. I start to look for the brown bag I saw Uhmma with earlier. I open the yellow plastic trash can. Empty. I pace up and down the length of the kitchen. I have to find that smell.

Outside, I notice the station wagon is gone from its usual spot on the street. We'll have to walk to Mrs. Song's, an ahjimma we met at church who lives a few miles away, for a ride. Uhmma refuses to let her pick us up for church even though we are right along the way. She does not want to inconvenience Mrs. Song more than she believes we already do.

Along the side of the house, Mr. Owner keeps two garbage cans, a black one for us and a brown one for him, just so we don't mix up our garbage and end up filling more than our allotted space. I pick up the lid of the black can and notice Uhmma's tight knot at the top of the white plastic trash bag. Just thinking about taking apart that knot makes me put the lid back down and walk away. After a few steps, I stop and kick the ground, spraying up the dust and loose gravel.

I go through the trash carefully, using an old cereal box to push through the mucky parts. By the second bag, I find it. An old rusted can of Country Fresh Lysol. I sit back on my legs and stare at the can. Why did Uhmma spray this? It explains the strange smell, but what about the brown paper bag? I lift out the white trash bags. At the bottom of the can is the brown paper bag. Now that I have found it, I am not sure that I want to look inside. I stand with my hands on my hips, staring down into the trash can, wondering if I should reach in and take it out.

"Uhn-nee."

Joon's voice startles me and makes me jump.

"What are you doing?" Joon asks.

"Joon," I say angrily, still feeling my heart pound, "what do you want?"

Joon leans forward and peeks into the trash can.

"Stop that," I say. "That's trash."

"So?" Joon shrugs and reaches in to pick up the brown paper bag. He peers inside, then pulls out an empty glass bottle with a white label that reads JIM BEAM and a red and blue Budweiser beer can. Joon sets them on the ground. Each time Joon reaches into the bag, he pulls out another Bud can. Soon a row of ten cans and the Jim Beam bottle line the wall.

"Is this what you were looking for?" Joon asks, staring at the lineup.

"No," I say. "I was only looking for the smell."

"You don't know the smell of this?" Joon says and stomps on one of the beer cans.

"Stop it, Joon."

Joon stomps on another can.

"That wasn't the smell," I say.

"Yeah, well, I don't care what you smelled in the house, it was just this crap again." Joon kicks the can so hard it bounces off the wall of the house and lands behind him. Joon runs after it and stomps it into the dirt. Sweat pours off his forehead, but Joon barely notices as he kicks the flattened can toward the trash. I run back inside the house.

Uhmma, I call, knocking quickly on the bedroom door and stepping inside. Uhmma sits on the bed, her body hunched forward, her head in her hands.

My breath catches. I want to believe they are shadows. Or a trick of the eye, like crouching shapes on dark, lonely streets that turn out to be trash cans up close. But they are not. The sickness in my stomach spreading up to my chest tells me they are real. Dark splotches of blue and purple camouflage Uhmma's bare back and shoulders. She tries to quickly pull on her sweater, but the sudden movement makes her gasp.

What do you want, Young Ju? Uhmma says harshly.

I open my mouth to speak, but the words are lost. I sit on the floor and begin to cry.

Uhmma does not move. She holds herself stiffly, waiting for me to stop.

Young Ju, go get ready for church, Uhmma says finally. Go now.

The footsteps of Mr. Owner shuffle across the ceiling. A fly buzzes above the bed, hitting its body over and over against a window sealed forever by too many layers of renter's paint.

I fiddle with the end of my shirt, trying to gather the courage to ask a question. I wipe my tears with my sleeve but remain sitting. Uhmma stands and moves to the small mirror on top of her dresser. She picks up her lipstick as though to finish putting on her makeup.

Why does Apa do it? I finally whisper and look to Uhmma for the answer.

Uhmma stares into the mirror, lipstick tight

in her hand. Young Ju, go now, Uhmma says.

But I will not leave this time. Will not pretend. The sight of the dark bruises, some as big as an iron across her back, lingers on the inside of my eyelids, each blink heavy with the weight of it all.

Why does Apa do it? I ask again, louder.

Uhmma slouches against the dresser. She puts down the lipstick. Uhmma says softly, There are some things you do not know about your Apa.

I wait for her to continue.

He is a very prideful man, Uhmma says.

So he has to hit us, I say and turn my face away.

Young Ju, you are too young to understand. Uhmma sighs deep from the source of her pain. He was so different when we first met, Uhmma says. He is still very upset over the death of your Halmoni.

That is no excuse, I say.

Uhmma doesn't respond. She dusts the dresser with her fingertips, adjusts the mirror. As Uhmma straightens the clutter of makeup on her dresser, she says, Your life can be different, Young Ju. Study and be strong. In America, women have choices.

I stand up. Stare straight at Uhmma. *You* have choices, Uhmma.

Uhmma refuses to meet my gaze. She looks

into the mirror and quickly applies some lipstick. When she lifts her arms to tie back her hair, a small groan escapes her lips. Aigoo. She lets her hair fall around her shoulders. I move up behind her, take the rubber band from her hand, and tie back her hair for her.

Uhmma turns around. She and I are almost the same height now. Her eyes sweep across my face, my hair. You are taller, she says, her voice trembling. You must have grown when I was not looking.

Patches

The middle school secretary calls for the second time this week. "Joon Park was not in school again today. He has been absent or tardy sixteen times this semester," she says. "He will flunk if he continues this pattern."

"Yes, I understand," I mumble into the phone.

But I don't understand. I don't know where Joon goes, what he does. Some days Joon does not come home until almost ten o'clock, just a few hours before Uhmma would catch him. He is becoming more like Apa, only wandering home when he needs sleep or food. I open the door to Joon's empty room. His red Korean mink blanket lies bunched together at the foot of the bed, his pillow pushed off to the ground. Sketches of his comic book heroes, X-Men, line the walls of his room. Crumpled drawings litter the floor. His drawings are surprisingly good. They have become better over time, since this is all he does when he's at home. Draw for hours behind his closed door, coming out only when he needs to eat.

A school picture of Joon when he was seven hangs above his desk. For some reason Uhmma had enough money that year to get a small individual photo, unlike the other years when all we brought home was the complimentary class picture. Joon's front teeth are almost completely rotten, but he flashes them for the camera as though they are made of gold. The cowlick on the side of his head sticks up in a nubby devil's horn.

The cowlick isn't there anymore; it got shaved off when Joon decided being bald and wearing black made him look tough. I check the room one more time and then close the door.

I am waiting on the couch when Joon comes home around dinnertime. He shuffles into the living room, dragging his feet and slouching with his head pushed forward in a new walk that reminds me of a vulture. Joon spots me on the couch and heads for his room. I call out, "Joon, come here."

"What do you want, Uhn-nee?" Joon says without turning around.

"I got a call from your school again."

Joon turns sideways, showing me his vulture profile. "You going to tell Uhmma?"

"Joon, where were you today? This was the second call this week. You know you're supposed to be at school."

170

"You can cut the lecture, Uhn-nee," Joon growls. "I don't need to hear it."

"Well, you can hear it from me or you can hear it from Apa."

Joon faces me fully, giving me an incredulous look. "You're going to tell Apa?"

"I don't want to," I say, playing with a loose thread on the yellow sheet covering the couch.

"Then don't. It's not like he's ever home anyway." Joon turns back around and walks to his room, shutting the door behind him.

I pull on the thread even though I know I shouldn't. Soon a small hole the size of a dime appears in the sheet. I sigh. We should get a new sheet anyway.

There is a dim crack of light escaping from under Joon's door. I knock, and as always there is no answer. I open the door anyway. Joon sits hunched over his desk. The light from his desk lamp makes the black bristles of his hair look even more sparse, like a landscape of trees in winter. I watch him from the door for a while and then make my way over to his desk.

Joon slowly traces the pencil sketches of his new drawing with a sharp black felt-tip marker. He finishes penning a small detail on Wolverine's leg muscle and finally looks up. "What do you want now, Uhn-nee?"

171

Up close, I notice that Joon's eyes are bloodshot, his eyelids heavy and drooping. I fight the impulse to reach up and touch his eyes, to check and make sure they really belong to Joon and not some sad grandfather, homeless and lying in the street. I stare at his drawing to avoid his eyes and ask, "Joon, where do you go when you skip class?"

Joon turns to another part of his drawing. "I hang out with my friends," Joon mumbles, trying to keep his hand steady.

"Well, what do you do?"

"What do you think we do? We goof around."

"All day?"

"God, Uhn-nee," Joon says, looking up from his work. "Why are you asking me all these questions? Why don't you skip school and find out for yourself if you're so curious."

"Joon, you know Uhmma and Apa want you to study and get good grades. What are you going to do when report cards come around?"

Joon's hand quivers for a second and the pen veers off the pencil sketch course. "Damnit, Uhn-nee! Look what you made me do." Joon goes over the line again, making the black outline wider in that one spot.

"Joon, did you hear me?"

"What do you want? *What!*" Joon slams the

pen down and turns in his seat to fully face me.

"You can't keep cutting school if you want to get decent grades," I say.

"Well, what if I don't want good grades? What if I don't want to be like you, Uhn-nee?"

"I'm not saying you have to be like me. I'm just saying you should be in school so you can learn something."

Joon snorts and picks up his pen again. "Yeah, real life lessons there."

"It's not like you're learning anything by goofing off with your friends."

"You don't even know what we do, so don't act like you're some expert, Uhn-nee. You don't know about a lot of things."

"Well, I know that if you skip school again, I'm going to tell Uhmma and Apa."

Joon's pen freezes in midair. He slowly turns in his chair, his eyes narrowed, the curl of a snarl frozen on his lips. "You squealing little pig."

"You don't have to get all nasty," I say, putting one hand on my hip.

"Get out of here and mind your own stupid nerdy business. You're probably jealous that I even have friends at school. Who are your friends, Uhn-nee? Who do you eat lunch with? The books at the library?"

I start to back out of the room. Joon stands up. "You have no friends of your own so you have to make me just like you. But I'm not like you. I have friends and at least I have fun when I'm not in this stupid apartment."

The anger of Joon's words forces me all the way to his door, ready to leave. But I can't. With the doorknob jammed against the small of my back, I watch Joon return to his drawing, his neck so tense and tight the back of his head touches his shoulders. The picture of the little rotten-toothed boy hangs above him. I stare at the picture and then look at Joon's hulking back. He is tall for his age. The tallest one in the family. Just like Apa and Uhmma thought he would be someday. The son who must make Apa proud. What has happened? Why have his eyes changed into those of someone so much older?

"Leave me alone, Uhn-nee," Joon mumbles.

"Please, Joon. Just go to school tomorrow," I say softly.

"I'll think about it," Joon answers.

I want to say more, ask him to try to go to school or else. But at the last minute I change my mind and simply leave his room. I let Joon lose himself to his drawings.

In the living room I finger the small hole that I unraveled in the sheet. I know there'll be no new sheet. No fresh, clean cover to make the old couch look better. Just this same sheet that has been here for as long as we have. I take out Uhmma's sewing kit and patch up the hole as best as I can.

Disclosure

Amanda and her mom drop me off at the library closest to my house after a Saturday study session for finals at Amanda's. I have been slowly seeing more of Amanda and telling Uhmma and Apa, if they ask, that I go to the library to study. Mrs. Doyle and Amanda joke every time they drop me off at the library that I practically live there. I laugh and say it's better than being in an empty house, and anyway, I can get my work done faster there without the distraction of the TV. They nod like they understand.

I get out quickly before Mrs. Doyle can ask about my parents, which has started to become a frequent question. She wants Uhmma to join the PTA. Come over and have lunch with a few of the other mothers. I've told her that Uhmma is busy, but Mrs. Doyle has not stopped asking.

Before closing the car door, I lean in and thank Mrs. Doyle for the ride.

"No problem, Young," Mrs. Doyle says easily. "Oh, Young, be sure to ask your mom if she can make it to lunch at our house next

Saturday. She can't be working every week-end."

I shrug. Uhmma has Saturday mornings and afternoons off, but I don't tell her that. I just smile awkwardly and say, "I'll ask."

After Amanda and her mom drive away, I start to walk home. Someday I might have to tell Amanda where I really live. Someday I'll tell her if we are still best friends.

I'm surprised to see Apa, instead of Uhmma, coming out of the kitchen after I shout out, Uhmma, I am back from the library.

Apa, I say, startled, and close the door behind me. Apa is supposed to be at his only remaining gardening job, but here he is in the middle of the living room, hands on his hips. Uhmma quietly comes out of the kitchen. I look back and forth between them.

Where were you just now? Apa asks with a squinty eye.

I slowly put down my backpack. The way he asks that question as though he already knows the answer makes me cringe inside. I stick with my story.

I was studying at the library, I say softly.

In two strides he is by my side, grabbing my hair and dragging me across the living room.

"Apa!" I scream and try to pull my hair from his grasp.

You bitch, he snarls. You lying bitch. Who do you think you are? Lying to my face!

Apa throws me on the couch and stands in front of me heaving, his nostrils flared, eyes thin with anger.

I bow my head slightly to keep from smelling the sour alcohol breath blowing down on my face, and instead find a spot on the far wall just behind Apa's brown belt. I keep my eyes focused on the spot.

Apa puts his hands on his hips. He says through clenched teeth, I saw you. I saw you at the library with that American girl. What did I tell you about seeing that worthless girl?

I think about asking him why he was at the library instead of at work, but instead I mumble, I do not remember.

Slap.

My ears ring and the side of my face grows numb.

How many times have you lied to me? Apa yells, stepping in closer.

I do not answer.

Slap.

The force of the blow knocks me sideways on the couch, the coolness of the yellow sheet pressing against my face. I want to close my eyes and pretend I have just fallen asleep in front of the television.

You. Lying. Bitch, Apa says in a low, slow voice. Going behind my back. I cannot even trust you to obey my orders.

I hold my hand over my face and stay lying on the couch. Apa grabs my hair again and pulls me up to a sitting position.

Give me that girl's number, Apa snarls. I will tell her she is not allowed to come near you again. I will tell her parents what kind of girl they have raised.

I find my spot and do not answer.

Give me her number.

No.

The rain of blows on my face, shoulders, and head forces my body to the ground. My hands slide into the shag carpet. I pretend I am drowning, letting the sea take me under. I close my eyes and the world cannot touch me.

You are going to kill her! Uhmma shouts.

Get away from me, woman, Apa growls. This is all your fault. Look at what kind of daughter you have raised, always lying and sneaking around. She is just like you. Apa kicks me in the stomach. I barely feel the blow. I am already floating away.

Yah, Uhmma screams. You worthless dog! You are no better than a common hoodlum. Why do you think our children hide from you all the time?

Liar, Apa roars.

When the blows stop and the sound of Uhmma's voice moves away from me, I slowly raise myself up on my elbows and squint at the blurred figures in my vision. I rub my eyes, trying to clear them of tears. Uhmma backs away toward the kitchen. Apa follows.

You and your sneaky ways. This is all your fault, Apa growls. Your fault.

Worthless dog! Uhmma screams. Hoodlum! Drunk bastard!

From the kitchen, the screams and shouts continue. The clanking of a pot hitting the floor jolts my body finally awake. I sit up and press my hands over my ears, close my eyes. The breaking comes inside, hitting, hitting my heart.

Stop, I whisper, rocking back and forth. Please, God, make it stop. Please. Please. God, make it stop. God. God?

A dull thud and Uhmma's scream halts my prayers. I open my eyes, and from somewhere inside my body, an answering scream finds its way out of my throat.

I don't think, just move. I lunge for the phone by the armchair. The three numbers are pressed so quickly I barely have time to hold the phone to my ear before a voice comes on, "Nine one one."

I'm shaking so badly I have to hold the receiver with both hands. The sound of the lady's voice on the other end asking "How may I help you?" almost makes me hang up. What am I doing? Do I really believe the police can help? That they care about me? They would not help people like us. I start to breathe too quickly and my vision blurs. For a second I forget I am still holding the phone against my ear.

"Hello?" the voice on the other end asks.

Do it, I tell myself. Speak. Save her. I can't. I start to cry.

"Hello? Hello?"

What am I doing? I look at the phone in my hand and let it drop to the ground. I hug my knees and rock, back and forth, back and forth. Halmoni's voice returns, Only God can. Only God can.

The sound of breaking and Uhmma's deep wail haunt the room. I pound my fist into my thigh and bite my lower lip. But I am not a child anymore. I do not have time to wait for God. There is only me. Stop it. Stop it. This is enough.

I pick up the phone and raise it to my ear. "Please," I whisper and take a gulp of air. "Send help."

"Tell me what is going on, miss."

"My father is killing my mother."

"Are you at one eight seven two La Madera Boulevard?"

I don't know how she knows this, but I'm thankful that I do not have to say more than "Yes." I clutch the phone tightly to my ear as another crash explodes the air. "Please, please," I whisper. "Hurry."

Seeds of Life

After the police handcuff Apa and take him away, Uhmma drives down to the police station with her face so badly bruised and misshapen an officer forces her to go to a hospital. Even after ten stitches on the cut above her eyebrow, two stitches on the corner of her lip, and taped ribs, Uhmma will not press charges. "My huh-su-bun," she tells them. I stand by her side translating, my voice breaking only once, when they ask if he beats me also. We are told to come back tomorrow. They must hold him for the night.

The next morning Uhmma and I wait in the car in front of the police station. Uhmma honks the horn when she sees Apa step outside. Apa barely glances in our direction. His eyes pass over us and stop at a point behind the car. A blue sedan that was parked not more than ten feet behind us starts its engine and drives by quickly, but not so fast that we cannot make out the figure of an Asian woman in the driver's seat. She stops the car at the curb. Apa walks quickly to the passenger's side. He steps in. They drive away.

Uhmma watches the sedan until it turns a corner and then disappears. After a few minutes of staring at the empty street, Uhmma finally turns on the ignition. The station wagon grumbles awake. But before she steps on the gas, Uhmma holds the steering wheel tightly with both chapped hands. She says to me with her eyes fixed on the road, This is all your fault.

The next few weeks, months, is a snowy blur. Uhmma hardly comes home. She works three jobs back to back, sleeping only during the dew-damp hours before dawn. Her body begins to waste away. Although every night I leave a bowl heaped with rice on the counter for her, every morning I find it sitting untouched. I empty the bowl back into the pot and replace the lid.

There is no more time for church. When school is out for the summer, Uncle Tim lies and says he needs Joon's and my help at his small ice cream shop on the beach. Joon complains all morning about missing stuff with his friends, but he's ready when Uncle Tim comes by to pick us up for work.

There isn't enough room for all three of us in the shop, so Joon stays outside sweeping the sidewalk of its endless sand while I stay inside pouring waffle mixture into a mold and burning my fingertips shaping the cones. Uncle Tim handles the customers. At the end of the day Uncle Tim gives us each thirty dollars and says we do good work. We thank him and pocket the money. At home, Joon gives me twenty of his. I use our money for the weekly groceries.

During these months, the only act that gives me comfort is rinsing the evening rice, my daily chore. I add the water to the pot of rice and push the heel of my hand against the rough grains. Push, swirl. Push, swirl. Almost instantly a white cloud of starch rises up and turns the water opaque. Murky. The grains disappear. For a moment, it seems like all that stands in the pot is a confusion of dirty water. But if I reach underneath the cloud, feel around, there they are. Tiny seeds waiting to be rinsed and exposed like nuggets of pearls.

One evening as I am washing the rice, my hand disappearing and reappearing in the murky cloud of starchy water, I hear the front door open and close, and then Uhmma is standing in the doorway of the kitchen.

Uhmma, I say loudly, startled to see her home early. Home at all. What are you doing home from the restaurant? I ask.

I am on my break, Uhmma says and comes over to stand beside me. She watches me clean the rice. My hands shake a little from having her observe me so closely.

When did you learn how to make the rice? she asks.

I shrug and pour out the milky water. I have watched you enough times, I say.

I suppose that was how I learned, she says. Watching my uhmma.

I finish rinsing the rice until the tiny grains are sitting in a pool of cold clear water. Uhmma takes the pot from my hands, wipes the wet bottom, and puts it into the rice cooker.

You have done a good job making the rice, Young Ju, Uhmma says.

I turn my face away from her. Blink rapidly at the far wall to keep my tears from spilling over. It has been a long time since she has spoken to me.

Young Ju, Uhmma says.

I refuse to look at her. Her hand touches my shoulder.

Young Ju, Uhmma says again.

"What," I answer gruffly, still refusing to meet her eyes.

Gomo came by the restaurant today, Uhmma says quietly. She came to give me a message. Apa is going back to Han Gook.

I look at Uhmma to see what that means to her. Now it is she who avoids my gaze.

Uhmma pats her cheek nervously and says, Gomo will borrow the money if we would like to go back with him.

I swallow hard.

Uhmma glances at me. I shake my head and begin cleaning the counter with a wet rag. I will not go, I say to myself. I will live with Amanda or something. Anything. Tears fall on the counter as quickly as I can wipe them away.

Uhmma takes the rag out of my hand. She reaches for my face and gently turns it away from the wall. I meet her eyes. Uhmma's face mirrors my own.

Please try to understand, Young Ju. These last few months have been difficult. I did not have the right words for you until today. I said things that are not true. I blamed you for my mistake. Uhmma shakes her head. I blamed you for trying to save me.

I want to reach out to Uhmma. Rest my head on her shoulder. But I stand in my place, arms crossed over my chest.

Uhmma says, Now it is my turn to do the right thing for you. For us. I told Gomo that we could take care of ourselves. My strong children and I will be fine without Apa.

I press my lips together, try to hold my breath, but the tears come anyway. I lower my chin and let them fall to the floor.

Uhmma smooths my forehead, my cheeks. Tucks my hair behind my ears like she used to do when I was young. I put my arms around her and rest my head on her shoulders.

She murmurs, You are my strong girl.

A Family of Dreamers

The patch of grass is so small you can walk across in four long strides. But I don't care. It is ours. I walk barefoot back and forth across the vibrant green lawn, take in deep breaths of air. My toes clutch the tiny blades, revel in the softness and the damp earth beneath my feet. All ours.

Young Ju, Uhmma calls from the bedroom window, come inside now. You can go out later. Uhmma smiles at me and shakes her head. Though we have boxes to unpack and a whole house to marvel at and clean, I can't get enough of this grass.

I shield my eyes from the bright sun and turn to look at the house we can finally call home. It's strange how much this home resembles the one in Korea. Same squat, square shape and low roof, like a sitting hen ready to lay. I suppose that was why Uhmma and I knew this would be the one from the moment we saw it. That and the tiny sliver of lawn in the backyard that I could see from the driveway. This house isn't in the best of neighborhoods or on top of a hill, and it needs new paint and some work on the windows and roof, but it's better than what we had all those years. All that time. With Apa.

It almost doesn't seem fair that I will have to leave for college in a few weeks. Before I have had the chance to memorize how long it takes for the hot water to come on or what sounds the house makes on rainy nights, or cut the grass when it becomes long and shaggy. Before I truly know this place, I will be gone. But Uhmma and Joon will love this house, grow into it until they can walk in their sleep to the bathroom. I bend down and run my fingers through the grass. And I will enjoy this lawn when I come home for the holidays.

The inside of the house is cool after the heat of the sun. Loud guitar music and the sound of hammering come from Joon's room. He is nailing up his drawings. Uhmma and I had a few framed one year for his birthday. Joon has promised I can take one to school with me. The kitchen floor is littered with boxes containing our dishes and pots, but the tile counters and cabinets smell of Windex and bleach. Uhmma has been here already.

Although Uhmma and I will have to share a bedroom when I'm at home, this house is bigger than the apartment. There is a living room separate from the dining room, something Uhmma did not know could exist. Even

Gomo and Uncle Tim have only one big room, a dining table at one end and the couch at the other. There are no boxes in our dining room. Only hard wooden floors and an intricate, diamond-shaped design in the middle of the ceiling. When we first looked at the house, Uhmma kept staring up at it, wondering what it was for. The agent told us that these old bungalows sometimes have nice detailing like that. He pointed to the middle of the diamond design and said, "That's where you would hang the chandelier." Now Uhmma dreams about getting a dining room table and a chandelier just like in the old movies with Cary Grant and Grace Kelly.

We still have the old couch, but there is a new blue sheet covering the cigarette burns. When Uhmma has enough money saved, she will look for a new couch. For now, this house has taken all our savings and more. All the money that Uhmma makes working at Gomo's new dry-cleaning business, the money from Joon's afterschool job at Kinko's, and my money from tutoring. Plus a loan that Uhmma could hardly make herself take from Uncle Tim and Gomo except that Gomo insisted because she said Uhmma was family.

But it was worth it. All of it. Luckily, I got a scholarship so Uhmma doesn't have to worry about paying for college. I twirl around the empty dining room and think about flying again. Going up, up, up. I spin around and around trying to make myself dizzy. Empty the fears that spring inside my head every time I think about leaving home. Uhmma and Joon. What if I don't like it at college? What if I stand out like an alien? What if I am disappointed?

I stop spinning. Get to work, I tell myself. Get busy. I pick up several boxes near the front door with Korean words scribbled on the sides and take them to Uhmma for deciphering. A few of the characters look familiar, but I never learned to read or write Korean.

Uhmma, I ask, turning the boxes around so she can read the writing, where do you want these?

Uhmma is sitting on the bed and arranging my clothes into neat piles for the dresser we will share. She looks up and squints at the words. Bring them in here, she says.

I drop them in front of her and have a seat on the bed. Uhmma pulls off the packing tape on the smaller box and opens it up. I lean forward to see what's inside.

Pictures. A pile of old black and white pictures. I can hardly believe my eyes. Here in this box is a fist-deep wealth of old memories.

Uhmma! I gasp. Where did you get those?

A gentle tug on the corners of her lips is all

the answer she will give me for now. Her face is almost sad. She lifts up a photo with an image of a young boy and an older girl dressed in matching blue uniforms.

Uhmma points to the girl, who looks about nine or ten. That is me, she says.

I take the picture from Uhmma. You? I ask and stare hard at the face. Same serious expression, a slight gathering of the eyebrows, lips held tightly closed, cheekbones high and prominent. I smile. Uhmma was determined even back then.

Who is that? I ask and point to the boy.

My brother, your uncle. Song Won Ju, Uhmma says, already picking out another photo.

The little boy is smiling so wide and open you can see his tongue. Why haven't I heard about Uhmma's brother? Or seen these photos? I vaguely remember a trip to visit Uhmma's parents, but their faces and the specifics of the visit are blurred and faint in my memory. I realize that a whole part of my history has been missing.

Uhmma, why have you not told us about your family? I ask.

Uhmma passes me another photo. This time I recognize Uhmma right away. She is a teenager, but her younger brother stands taller. He's even taller than his father. He is as tall as Joon. The four of them are dressed formally. Uhmma and her mother stand in low pumps, wearing dark dresses and long woolen coats with fur on the collar. The men are in suits and ties. Even with the countryside in the background, there is an air of wealth about them.

I pull on Uhmma's shoulder. Why have you not shown me these photos? I ask.

This time Uhmma stops going through the pictures. She sighs and slouches back. Wisps of hair have escaped from her bun. These pictures, Uhmma says, waving her hand at the box, are hard for me to look at.

What do you mean? I ask.

They remind me too much of Han Gook. My family. They make me homesick.

Why did you not let Joon and me look at them?

Uhmma glances at me sideways. Your Apa would not have been happy to know I had kept these with me.

Why?

Uhmma smiles and says, It is always why with you, Young Ju.

I shrug.

Because, Uhmma says and pats my hand. Apa did not like to be reminded of where I came from.

I slowly hold up the picture of Uhmma and

her family. Because you were rich, I state.

Uhmma stares down at her hands. We sit silent for a moment, and then Uhmma reaches into the box again and pulls out another photo.

This one is for you, she says.

I take it from her, glance at the young man holding a little girl on his shoulders and at the woman standing by his side. Waves and a long stretch of beach lie in the background.

Is this when you were young? I ask.

No, Young Ju, Uhmma says. Look again.

This time I study the man carefully. Study the slope of his nose, the way his eyes crinkle in the corners from his broad grin like the eyes of sleepy cats in the sun. The way his hair stands up straight in the front from a cowlick. Then I look at the little girl. She is not facing the camera. Instead, her head is turned slightly, her eyes watching the waves. The woman grins broadly at the man.

I carefully point to the little girl. That is me.

Uhmma points to the man and woman. And Apa and me, she says softly. That was one of the best days I can remember.

I try to think back. Remember. The waves. Uhmma! I exclaim, a memory forming on the edge of my tongue. You taught me how to jump in the waves that day.

Uhmma wrinkles her eyebrows together,

shakes her head slightly.

Was it Halmoni? I ask. Halmoni loved the beach, I say.

Uhmma leans in close. It was your Apa, Young Ju.

I frown. Apa?

He loved the waves, Uhmma says. I remember how worried I was to see you go into the water. But somehow he taught you to be brave that day. You loved the waves after that. Never wanted to come out.

Apa?

What dreamers you two, were! Pretending to be dolphins, then seals, then ships that could sail far across the sea. Uhmma suddenly turns away from me, looks out the window of our new home. After a moment she says quietly, He was a different man back then.

I trace the faces in the picture with my fingertips. I can barely remember the feel of his arms as he held me tight and asked me to be brave. How scared I was of the waves, of what might be out there.

You take that with you, Uhmma says, peering over my shoulder. Take it to college so you can remember how to be brave. She holds the corner of the picture for a second and then lets go. Uhmma turns her face to the window again. She gazes out and says quietly, And remember, Young Ju. You come from a family of dreamers.

I hold the picture close to my heart.

I am a sea bubble floating, floating in a dream. Bhop.

Epilogue: Hands

Uhmma's hands are as old as sand. They have always been old, even when we were young. In the mornings, they would scratch across our sleeping faces as she smoothed our foreheads, our cheeks, and told us quietly, Wake up. Time for school.

At work, her hands sewed hundreds of jeans before the lunch bell sounded and then boxed hundreds more before she left for her night job at Johnny's Steak House. They knew how to make a medium-rare steak, baked potato on the side, in ten minutes flat for hungry customers always in a hurry.

Uhmma's hands washed our dinner dishes, cleaned the kitchen floor with a rag, folded load after load of laundry. They could raise hems of second-hand dresses with stitches so tiny there was barely a line. Even on Sunday they held a Bible and helped set out dough-nuts and coffee after the service. Uhmma's hands rarely rested.

But sometimes, not often — and not when Uhmma was tired and wanted only to feel the cool underside of a pillow — but sometimes, her hands would open. Sitting cross-legged on the carpet, in a sunspot bright as the open sea, Uhmma unfurled her fingers. Palms up. A flower finally open to the bees.

Joon and I would rush to sit on either side of her. Uhmma held our small hands in her own and said she could read stories in the lines of our palms.

Look, Young Ju, Uhmma said. Your intelligence line is strong. Someday, maybe you will become a doctor. Uhmma traced the line with her cat-tongue finger, tickling my hand as it moved from the heel of my palm up to the base of my middle finger.

Joon shoved away my hand and offered his for inspection. Look at my intelligence line, Uhmma.

These baby hands have lines? Let me see, Uhmma said and brought his palm up close to her face. She studied it for a moment and then suddenly kissed the middle. Plop. A raindrop on water.

Joon giggled, kicking out his feet. This one, Uhmma. Tell me about this one, Joon said and pointed to a line on his palm, the one that predicted he would live to be an old, successful man with many children.

It did not matter that we had heard the stories before. Each telling was a lullaby of dreams we never wanted to wake from. We were reaching, always reaching, to touch Uhmma's sandpaper palms.

Uhmma said her hands were her life. But for us, she only wished to see our hands holding books. You must use this, she said and pointed to her mind. Uhmma's hands worked hard to make sure our hands would not resemble hers.

It takes only a glance at our nails, our knuckles, our palms to know Uhmma succeeded. Joon and I both possess Uhmma's lean fingers, but without the hard, yellowed calluses formed by years of abuse from physical labor. Our hands turn pages of books, press fingertips to keyboard buttons, hold pencils and pens. They are lithe and tender. The hands of dreams come true.

As I walk with Uhmma now, her hand grasped firmly in mine, I can feel the strength that was there in our childhood ebbing away. I cup her hand, unfurl her fingers, and let the lines of her palm speak to the sky. They are the marks of story and time. For some it might be hard to tell which lines were there from birth and which ones immigrated from countless jobs. But I can tell.

I trace a set of tiny lines etched along her thumb. They speak of Uhmma's early years gathering and drying fish along the Korean coastline. I follow another path and find a deep groove at the base of her pointer finger. Immediately I smell the smoky kitchen of the steak house crowded with visitors just pulling off the I-5 for dinner.

Too busy, she had explained as she unwound the Reynolds plastic wrap and tried to peel away the blood-soaked napkin from the cut. The old scar, white and fleshy, still remembers the hard kiss of the dancing knife.

I smooth the tips of her fingers. Tiny flecks of skin, parched from dry-cleaning clothes, ironing shirts, "heavy on the starch," stand up searching for the moisture that was robbed day after day for eleven years.

In the middle of her palm, the creases are still strong. Although the line of riches is cut short by a scar from an unseen hook caught in a fish's mouth, her lifeline extends out full and long. The marriage line is faint, crisscrossed by tiny cracks in the skin starting and ending in a mystery. Uhmma's hands have lived many lives, though her hair only recently has begun to gray.

I study these lines of history and wish to erase them. Remove the scars, the cuts, fill in the cracks in the skin. I envelop Uhmma's hands in my own tender palms. Close them together. Like a book. A Siamese prayer. I tell her, I wish I could erase these scars for you.

Uhmma gently slips her hands from mine.

She stares for a moment at her callused skin and then says firmly, These are my hands, Young Ju. Uhmma tucks a wisp of my long, straight black hair behind my ear and then puts her arm around my waist. We continue our walk along the beach.